AB

Caroline Anderson is a matriarch, writer, armchair gardener, unofficial tearoom researcher and eater of lovely cakes. Not necessarily in that order! *What Caroline loves:* her family. Her friends. Reading. Writing contemporary love stories. Hearing from readers. Walks by the sea with coffee/ice cream/cake thrown in! Torrential rain. Sunshine in spring/autumn. *What Caroline hates:* losing her pets. Fighting with her family. Cold weather. Hot weather. Computers. Clothes shopping. *Caroline's plans:* keep smiling and writing!

Also by Caroline Anderson

Yoxburgh Park Hospital miniseries

The Secret in His Heart
Risk of a Lifetime
Best Friend to Wife and Mother?
Their Meant-to-Be Baby
The Midwife's Longed-For Baby
Bound by Their Babies
Their Own Little Miracle

Discover more at millsandboon.co.uk.

THEIR OWN LITTLE MIRACLE

CAROLINE ANDERSON

MILLS & BOON

First published in Great Britain 2018
by Mills & Boon, an imprint of HarperCollins*Publishers*
1 London Bridge Street, London, SE1 9GF

Large Print edition 2019

© 2018 Caroline Anderson

ISBN: 978-0-263-07802-2

MIX
Paper from
responsible sources
FSC® C007454

This book is produced from independently certified FSC™ paper to ensure responsible forest management. For more information visit www.harpercollins.co.uk/green.

Printed and bound in Great Britain
by CPI Group (UK) Ltd, Croydon, CR0 4YY

For everyone who's struggled with infertility
or faced the anguish of childlessness,
and for those who've had the courage
to act as surrogate or donor and given
such a priceless gift.

CHAPTER ONE

'ED TRAUMA CALL, ten minutes.'

Iona's heart sank. Another one? The previous trauma patient had only just arrived, and they were seriously short-staffed. Andy Gallagher was on holiday, Sam Ryder had gone for lunch five minutes ago at three thirty, they were rushed off their feet and she was virtually on her own because James Slater, the clinical lead, was already up to his eyes in Resus with the trauma patient who'd just arrived, a construction worker with severe crush injuries to his chest who from what she could gather was resisting all attempts to resuscitate him.

Which made her, a brand new registrar, the most senior doctor available, so it wasn't a surprise when she was called into Resus. James didn't pause what he was doing. 'Iona, can you take the trauma call, please? I can't leave my patient but I'll be right here, so you can run things by me if you need to.'

'Sure.'

She went back to her patient, handed her over to the F2 junior doctor she was with, found out as much detail as possible about the incoming casualty, went into Resus and put on a lead apron. Their patient had been hit by a car and had suspected pelvic injuries, which she really hadn't wanted to hear, so he'd need X-rays to check for fractures. She hoped they wouldn't be too serious because James was still tied up and looking at him she was fairly sure he would be for some time, because he and his team were now opening the patient's chest and it wasn't looking pretty.

Around her a new team was assembling: Tim, an F1 junior doctor fresh out of medical school who was totally out of his depth, Jenny, thankfully a highly competent nurse, Sue, a radiographer she trusted, ready with the portable X-ray and ultrasound, another nurse who she'd worked with in the past and who seemed OK, and a recently qualified health care assistant as the scribe.

Well, she just hoped the patient wasn't too bad, because as teams went, this one was inadequate on several fronts. Not Sue, though, who was already surrounding the bay with lead screens, and not Jenny. Just her, Tim and the HCA, then. It was a good job James was right beside them, even if he was up to his eyes.

She briefed them quickly on what little she knew, allocated them their positions in the team and made sure they were ready. 'Right, lead and plastic aprons, please, everyone, and you all know what you're doing?' she checked, then it was too late to worry because the patient was being wheeled in and they were given the handover by the paramedics.

'This is Jim Brown, age fifty-six, hit on his right-hand side by a large van about forty minutes ago, suspected pelvic injury. We put a pelvic binder on and secured his spine at the scene. BP one-twenty over eighty, sats ninety-eight per cent, we've given him ten of morphine and started him on saline. No apparent head or chest trauma but he's complaining of pain in the right wrist so we've splinted it.'

The pelvic injury wasn't good news, but at

least his blood pressure was all right so hopefully he could be transferred to Orthopaedics shortly. 'OK, everybody, can we get these clothes off so I can do a primary survey, please? Sue, we need a FAST scan, and somebody book an urgent CT? Jenny, take bloods, cross match for four units, and we'll have packed cells and FFP on standby, please. Sue, after the FAST scan I'd like X-rays of C-spine, chest and pelvis. And make a note of the time. Fifteen forty-six.'

The team went into action and she bent over the patient so she was in his line of sight; he was conscious but in obvious pain and distress, and she smiled reassuringly at him. 'Hello, Jim. My name is Iona, I'm a doctor and I'm going to be looking after you. Can you tell me where it hurts?'

'All down there—don't know, it's all blurred together.'

'Anything else? Head? Chest?'

'No, they're fine. My right wrist hurts, that's all.'

'OK.' She looked up at the monitor to check his blood pressure. One-ten over seventy, slightly down. She'd need to keep a close eye on it. 'How's the FAST scan, Sue?'

'Some free fluid in the abdomen,' Sue murmured softly. Which was highly suggestive of a pelvic fracture. And his blood pressure had dropped since the paramedics had reported it.

They stepped back briefly so Sue could X-ray his pelvis for confirmation, then Iona shut her mind to everything else and concentrated on Jim. Pupils equal and reactive, airway clear, good bilateral breath sounds, no significant pain when she felt his chest, no obvious bumps on his head, but his right wrist was almost certainly fractured.

And so was his pelvis. The X-ray showed multiple fractures of the pelvic ring, some displaced. No wonder he was bleeding, but hopefully his neck and chest were clear and he still had circulation to both feet. Small mercies, she thought.

'Right, Jenny, can we start the PRBC and FFP, and can someone page Orthopaedics please? Multiple pelvic fractures. Sue, can you get the neck and chest shots, please.'

'If he's got pelvic fractures you need to page IR,' James said over his shoulder, and she took a breath and nodded. At least he was listening and keeping her on track. She could do this.

'OK. Can someone page Interventional Radiology as well, please? How about CT, James?'

'No, wait for IR. They'll probably take him straight to the IR suite to embolise the damaged arteries.'

If she was lucky…

She was scanning the X-rays when she heard the swish of the door opening and closing behind her. She glanced round to see who it was, and her heart did a funny little hitch. The interventional radiologist? He didn't look old enough to be a consultant, but he had the firm tread of someone who knew what he was doing. She could only hope—

'Hi. I'm Joe Baker, IR Specialist Registrar. You've got a pelvic fracture for me?'

She met his eyes and her head emptied. Framed by the longest, darkest lashes, they were very pale blue, almost azure, with a dark rim. Utterly gorgeous and curiously penetrating. Mesmerising, in fact…

She gave herself a mental kick and tried to focus. 'Yes. Hi. I'm Iona Murray, Registrar. This is Jim Brown, fifty-six years old, hit by a car on the right, BP one-twenty over eighty on admission, now...' her eyes flicked to the monitor, and her heart sank '...ninety-five over sixty. Sats were ninety-eight per cent, now ninety-six. FAST scan shows free fluid, X-ray confirms multiple fractures of the pelvic ring. I think the chest and neck are clear but they haven't been checked by a radiologist.'

He nodded and held out his hand. 'May I?' He took the tablet from her, scrolled through the images and frowned. 'Right, they are clear but the pelvis is a mess and I'll need to embolise him. Has he had a CT yet?'

'No. We haven't had time.'

'How's his airway? Any obvious chest trauma or signs of head injury? Cardiac tamponade? Pleural effusion?'

'No.'

'Are you leading?' he asked, and she nodded.

'Right, I'll take over from here. Go on.'

She didn't know whether to be relieved or furious, because frankly it was a close-run thing. She went for relieved.

'He's also got a query fracture of right radius and ulna, but good cap refill and sensation.'

'OK, that can wait, then, so can the CT. Can you cancel the slot, please, if you've booked it, and alert IR?'

Joe reached for his neck, then frowned. 'Stethoscope?' he said briskly, holding out his hand, and she lifted her stethoscope over her head and handed it to him reluctantly.

'You're dead meat if anything happens to it, it was a graduation present from my sister,' she muttered darkly, and he rolled his eyes, introduced himself to Jim and checked his chest.

'OK, his chest's clear so I'll take him straight to IR—'

'BP falling. Sixty-five over forty.'

Jim was crashing. He groaned, and Iona took his hand.

'It's OK, Jim, we're here, we've got you,' she said, squeezing his hand for reassurance. But it was cold and lifeless, clammy now as well, and she felt her pulse spike.

'Right, can we have the REBOA kit, please, we need to do this now,' Joe said. 'And get me an arterial kit before we lose the femoral artery.'

He was going to insert a balloon into his aorta in *Resus*? Her eyes widened. She'd never seen it done, far less assisted, and she felt a moment of panic.

'I can page Sam,' Iona said hopefully. Sam, who was an ex-army medic, had done it dozens of times in the field and would know exactly what to do, but Joe Baker wasn't waiting.

'No time. Can I have a pair of scissors? The first thing we need to do is cut a chunk out of the pelvic binder to give me access.'

He cut a slit above the femoral artery on Jim's left leg and removed a V from the fabric with a deft snip of the scissors. 'First I'm going to secure access to the CFA so we don't lose it. I'm going in on the left because the fractures are worse on the right, so this is our best chance,' he explained, searching for the artery with his gloved fingertips, his hands rock steady. 'OK, Jim, sharp scratch coming,' he warned as he inserted the needle, but Jim was beyond noticing.

'Right, we're in. Someone open the REBOA pack and cover him in the sterile drapes. Just leave the site accessible, please. Iona, you're assisting, come and scrub.'

She felt her pulse rate go up another notch. The IR was already scrubbing and she followed him, joining him at the sink. 'Isn't it dangerous without imaging?' she asked under her breath as she scrubbed. 'You can't see what's going on in there. Wouldn't it be safer in the IR suite?'

He skewered her with those mesmerising eyes, and they'd turned to ice. 'Are you questioning my clinical competence?'

She held the icy stare with difficulty and shook her head. 'No, no, not at all! I'm questioning mine. I've never assisted with one of these—'

'Well, here's your chance, because he won't make it to IR and if we don't do this now, we'll lose him, so I suggest you take a deep breath and get on with it, because frankly he doesn't have time for this and nor do I. What do you know about a Zone III REBOA?'

She searched her brain, her heart hammering. 'It stands for Resuscitative Endovascular Balloon Occlusion of the Aorta, and it's a balloon catheter inserted via the common femoral artery to cut off the blood supply from the aorta below the balloon. Zone III occlusion is below the renal and mesenteric vessels, and it stops the bleeding from the damaged arteries in the pelvis, so it'll keep his heart and brain alive until you can get him into the IR suite or Theatre and stop the bleeding.'

'Contraindications?'

'Chest trauma, cardiac tamponade, pneumothorax, haemothorax, pleural effusion, aortic dissection—'

'OK, we've ruled them out, so what are the dangers?'

'Damage to the femoral artery or aorta, and reperfusion injury from cutting off the blood supply for too long.'

He nodded. 'Exactly, so time is of the essence. Right, let's get on with this.'

She swallowed and sucked in a breath and reached for a paper towel as someone helped him into a sterile gown. 'What do you want me to do?'

'Get gowned up.' He crossed to the bed, snapping on gloves as he went. 'OK, we're ready. Let's go.' Jim was completely covered with the sterile drapes, leaving just the small area with the cannula sticking out uncovered for access. He glanced at the team as he reached for the

REBOA trolley and injected a local around the site of the cannula, then flushed it with heparinised saline and inserted a fine guide wire.

'Someone phone the IR suite and get them on standby for immediate transfer as soon as I'm done,' he said as he was working. 'Tell them I'll be ten minutes. OK, Iona, watch and learn.'

She watched, and she learned how wrong she'd been to doubt him. His hands were steady and confident, sensitive as he removed the cannula from the guide wire and inserted the large bore introducer with great care. 'This is the tricky bit,' he said. 'You don't want to tear the artery, and the Twelve French makes a damn great hole, so you have to be subtle. OK, that's good.' He pulled out the fine wire and threaded the stiff guide wire in to the mark he'd made by holding it up against Jim's body. Hence the gowns and extensive drapes, she realised, so he could do that without risk of contamination of the wire.

'Right, it's in. Can you hold that steady, please, Iona, I don't want it to move. Keep an eye on the mark on it. Good. X-ray check, please, around T4.' He watched the screen, then nodded. 'OK, that's good. Then I slide the balloon catheter in over it, up to the mark, which is below the end of the guide wire, and then I inflate—like that, until I feel the resistance change,' he said, squeezing the syringe steadily to fill the balloon with saline.

'OK, that should be it. X-ray check here, please,' he said, indicating the level.

His eyes flicked to the clock, then the monitor, then the X-ray screen, and she saw the tension go out of his shoulders. 'Good. His BP's picking up. Time sixteen seventeen. Make sure that's on the notes, please. Right, secure this lot with a grip-lock dressing so nothing moves, and let's go. The clock's ticking and we've got an hour, max.'

Moments later the doors swished shut behind them, and as the team dispersed Iona stood there amid the litter of the procedure, staring after them in a mixture of bewilderment and awe.

Had all that only taken thirty-one minutes? It had been the longest half-hour of her life, but Joe Baker seemed to have taken it in his stride, not seeming even slightly fazed by it.

Good luck, or good judgement? Maybe a bit

of both, but Jim was still alive and she knew if it hadn't been for Joe they would have lost him.

It wasn't going so well for James and his team, though, from what she could hear, and definitely not his patient.

Then she heard James sigh heavily. 'OK, everyone, I'm calling it. Are we all agreed?' There was a low murmur, followed by silence. 'Time of death, sixteen twenty-one. Can somebody cover him, please, but leave everything in place for the post mortem. I'll go and talk to his family.'

Her eyes flicked to James, and he was stripping off his gloves and gown and coming over to her.

She smiled at him sympathetically. 'Thanks for your support. I'm sorry about your patient.'

'Yeah, me, too, but that's life. You did well, by the way. Are you OK?'

She smiled properly this time, slightly surprised to find that she was, even though she was shaking from head to foot. 'Yes, I am. He was quite hard on me, but I probably deserved it. I was freaking out a bit, but he made it look so easy.'

James smiled. 'I've heard great things about

Joe. He's only been here a few weeks, but his clinical lead says he's red hot, and he thinks he'll go far.'

'Unlike me. I was like a rabbit in headlights.'

'No, you weren't, you were just faced with a dying patient and no real way of dealing with it, even though you were doing everything right. Sam couldn't have got here in time, and if Joe hadn't been here you would have lost him, or I would have had to abandon my patient to save yours. Not that it would have mattered, as it turns out. Sometimes we just can't save them.'

She swallowed. 'I know.' She stripped off her gown and gloves, dumped them in the bin, took off the heavy lead apron and realised her stethoscope, her anchor that reminded her on an hourly basis that she really was a doctor and it wasn't just a dream, wasn't there. And Joe had already mislaid his own.

'Rats. He's still got my stethoscope.'

'They'll have one on the desk. You'll get it back.'

She smiled grimly. 'Too right I will. Thanks, James.'

He pushed open the door. 'You're welcome.

Right, I need to talk to my patient's family, and you need to talk to yours. Ah, here comes the cavalry. You've just missed Iona's first REBOA, Sam.'

Sam's eyes widened and he looked at Iona. '*You* did it?'

'No, of course I didn't, I just assisted. Joe Baker came down and he was going to take him to IR, but then the patient crashed and it was— he did it, just like that.'

'Of course he did. That's all they do in IR, stick things in blood vessels. It's their job. I should damn well hope he was good at it. Did he talk you through it?'

'Yes—once he'd lectured me for doubting him.'

Sam laughed. 'Yeah, that wouldn't have gone down well.'

'It didn't. He got his own back, though. He's nicked my stethoscope.'

'The one your sister gave you?' He chuckled. 'He's a brave man. I suggest you go and look for a nice quiet ingrowing toenail until it's time to go home. That should keep you out of mischief. And don't worry, you'll get it back.'

* * *

He still had her stethoscope.

The graduation present from her sister, the one he'd been told in no uncertain terms not to lose or damage. He could see why, it was a really expensive one, although it had to be a few years old now. No wonder she'd been precious about it. His own was only slightly better, and he'd bought it last year because he'd mislaid the one identical to this.

That was getting to be a habit.

He changed out of his scrubs, pulled on his clothes, clipped his watch on his wrist and checked the time. Seven thirty. She'd be long gone, unless she was on a late shift, but it was worth a try. He might even invite her out for dinner—assuming she'd speak to him. He'd been a bit tough on her, but he felt a grudging admiration for a junior registrar who'd had the guts to stand up to him in defence of her patient.

He headed down to the ED, found the nurse who'd been with them in Resus and asked her where Iona was.

She folded her arms and looked him straight

in the eye, and he had the distinct feeling he was in trouble. 'She's gone.'

'Do you know where I can find her? I borrowed her stethoscope and forgot to give it back.'

'Yes, she mentioned that. She wasn't happy about it.'

He laughed softly. 'No, I'm sure she wasn't.'

'You can leave it with me.'

'I can't do that. She told me I'd be dead meat if anything happened to it and I don't think it was an empty threat. I'll hang onto it and give it to her tomorrow.'

'She's away this weekend. She's not back in till Monday.'

'And I'm on a course next week. Great.' He hesitated. 'I don't suppose you know her address or mobile number?'

Jenny raised an eyebrow. 'Now, you don't seriously expect me to give it to you? I do know where you can find her, though. She's at the Queens Hotel just round the corner. There's a charity speed-dating event raising money for the new IR angio-surgical suite. I'm surprised you aren't going anyway as it's in aid of your department, but here's your chance to support it. Out of the drive, turn left, five hundred yards on the right. You can't miss it.'

Speed-dating? Seriously? She was gorgeous! Why would she need to go speed-dating, of all things? And then he realised she'd be helping with the organisation. Idiot.

'OK. Thanks.' He headed for his car, followed the directions and parked on the road opposite the hotel. The speed-dating event was signposted from Reception, and he headed towards the door. It shouldn't be hard to find her—

'Oh, excellent, we're short of men, especially good-looking young doctors. That'll be ten pounds, please. Can I take your name?'

He frowned. 'How do you know I'm a doctor?'

'The stethoscope?'

'Ah. Yes. Actually—' He was about to tell the woman why he was there, and then spotted Iona at one of the tables that were arranged in a circle, a man sitting opposite her. OK, she wasn't just helping, she was actually doing it as well, and if he wanted to see her, he'd have to pay up and queue for his slot. That was fine. It meant she'd have to listen to him for three minutes or whatever it was, which meant he'd have time to apologise for pushing her so far out of her comfort zone in Resus. And having three minutes to look at her was no hardship. He might even persuade her to go out for dinner—

'Name, please?'

'Sorry. Joe Baker. I've only got a twenty-pound note,' he said, but the woman just smiled, said, 'That'll do perfectly,' plucked it out of his fingers, stuck a label with 'JOE' written on it on his chest and handed him a printed card and a pencil.

So he could score the ladies? Good grief. He wrote her name and ten out of ten, and waited.

There was a gap before Iona, maybe because of the lack of men, so he hovered and then pounced when the bell rang and the man at her table got up and moved on.

He sat down in front of her, and she looked up from her score card and did a mild double take, her eyes widening.

'What are *you* doing here?'

He took the stethoscope from round his neck and handed it to her with a rueful smile. 'I forgot to return this, and when I refused to give it to the nurse who was in Resus because you'd told me in no uncertain terms what you'd do to me, she told me where to find you.'

Her mouth flickered in a smile. 'Ah. Jenny.'

'Yeah, that's right. She wouldn't give me your address.'

Her eyes widened. 'I should hope not!'

He gave a little huff of laughter at the outrage in her voice. 'I might have been insulted if I hadn't been glad she was so protective of your privacy, but I also wanted to apologise for pushing you out of your comfort zone in Resus.'

'You don't need to apologise,' she said, her clear and really rather lovely green eyes clouding, 'even though you were rude and patronising—'

'Rude and patronising?' he asked, pretending to be outraged, but she held his eyes and a little smile tugged at her mouth, drawing his attention to it. Soft, full, and very expressive. Like her eyes. He wondered what it would be like to kiss her—

'You were a teeny bit. I was way out of my comfort zone, because I thought you'd need more from me than I could give you. I've never led before on a case that critical and I should have appreciated you'd only do what you knew you could, but I was afraid Jim was going to die and I was freaking out a bit. I'm sorry you took it wrong, it really wasn't meant like that.'

'Don't apologise,' he said wryly. 'Standing up to me took guts, and you were quite right about the risks. Without image guidance there were no guarantees I could get the guide wire in without causing more damage, but I'd had a good look at the X-rays and I was pretty sure I could do it, and anyway, as I think I pointed out fairly succinctly, Jim had run out of options. He's OK, by the way. I sorted the bleeds, repaired the entry site and shipped him off to the orthos with a nice healthy reperfusion and well within the time limit. They've put an ex-fix on in Theatre and he's doing OK.'

He saw her shoulders sag slightly with relief. 'Oh, good. Thanks for the update. I've been worrying about him.'

'No need to worry, he's sore, he's broken but he'll make it. Good stethoscope, by the way. Very good. Your sister must think a lot of you.'

She smiled, her eyes softening. 'She does. That's why I was worried about you walking off with it, knowing you'd already lost yours. It didn't bode well.'

He laughed at that little dig. 'I hadn't *lost* it, it was in my locker, I just failed to pick it up—but I did lose the last one, so you weren't wide of the mark. You did well, by the way,' he added, sliding his score sheet across the table to her. 'It was a tricky case to manage and you'd done everything right. You should be proud of yourself.'

She glanced down at the paper and her eyes widened. 'Ten out of ten? That's very generous. You must be feeling guilty.'

'No, I just give credit where it's due, even if I *am* rude and patronising. And I did return your stethoscope, so hopefully that'll earn me a few Brownie points.'

'Maybe the odd one.'

Her lips twitched, and he sat back with a smile, folded his arms and held her eyes, trying not to think about kissing her. Or peeling off that clingy little top and—

'So, anyway, that's why I'm here. What about you?'

'Me?' She looked slightly flustered. 'Because it's a good cause?'

He raised an eyebrow at her, deeply unconvinced, and she smiled and shrugged and took him completely by surprise. 'OK. You asked. I'm looking for a sperm donor.'

Joe felt his jaw drop, and he stifled the laugh in the nick of time. Of all the unlikely things for her to say, and to him, of all people...

'You're kidding.'

'No. No, I'm not kidding. I'm looking for a tall Nordic type with white-blond hair, blue eyes and good bone structure, so you can relax, you don't qualify.'

'I might feel a bit insulted by that,' he said, still trying to work out if she was joking.

She smiled, her eyes mocking. 'Oh, don't be, it's not personal. I have very specific criteria and you don't fit them.'

He frowned at her, but she was so deadpan he didn't know whether she was completely off her trolley or winding him up. He turned and scanned the men in the room and this time he didn't stifle the laugh.

'OK,' he murmured in a low undertone. 'Nor does anyone else in this room. So far you've written zero out of ten against everyone, and the nearest candidate is white-blond because he's twice your age. He's also about three inches shorter than you and twice as heavy. And the lady on the next table looks *utterly* terrifying, so frankly I reckon we're done here. I'm starving, I haven't eaten since breakfast and I don't suppose you have, either, so why don't we get the hell out of here, go and find a nice pub and have something to eat? And that way I can apologise properly for being *rude and patronising.*'

'Won't your wife mind?' she asked, clearly fishing, and he raised an eyebrow and gave her the short answer.

'I don't have one. So—dinner?'

She hesitated for so long he thought she was going to say no, but then the bell rang, the lady at the next table was eyeing him hungrily, and she looked at the man heading to take his place, grabbed her bag and stethoscope and got to her feet.

'Sorry. We have to go,' she said, squeezing round from behind the table, and they headed for the door amid a chorus of protests. From both sexes. He stifled a smile.

'Right, where to?' he asked, and she shrugged.

'What do you fancy? Thai, Chinese, Mexican, Indian, Asian fusion, pub grub, Italian, modern British—'

'Good grief. All of those in Yoxburgh?'

She chuckled. 'Oh, yes. They might be busy, though, it's Friday night.'

He had a much better idea. 'How about a nice, cosy gastro-pub? There's one right round the corner from my house that comes highly recommended, and we'll definitely get a table there.'

'Is it far? Can I walk back? My car's at home.'

'No, it's a bit out of town, but that's fine, I'll drive you home. Look on it as a hire charge for the use of your stethoscope.'

Again she hesitated, a wary look in her eyes, but then she nodded as if she'd finally decided she could trust him. 'OK. That sounds good.'

To her surprise—and slight consternation—he headed out of town and turned off the main road down a lane so small it didn't even have a signpost.

'Where are we going?' she asked, wondering if she should be worried and trying to convince herself that she shouldn't, that he was a doctor, he was hardly going to harm her—

'Glemsfield,' he said. 'It's a tiny village, but it has a great pub and a thriving little community.'

'It's in the middle of nowhere,' she said. Even quieter than where her parents lived, and that was pretty isolated. And it was getting dark. Was she mad? Or just unable to trust any man to have a shred of decency?

'It is. It's lovely, and it's only three miles from Yoxburgh and much more peaceful. Well, apart from the barking muntjac deer at night. They get a bit annoying sometimes but I threaten them with the freezer.'

That made her laugh. 'And does it work?'

'Not so you'd notice,' he said drily, but she could hear the smile in his voice.

They passed a few houses and dropped down into what she assumed must be the centre of the village, but then he drove past the brightly lit pub on the corner, turned onto a drive and cut the engine.

Although it was only dusk the area was in darkness, shrouded by the overgrown shrubs each side of the drive, and the whole place had a slight air of neglect. She suppressed a shudder of apprehension as she got out of the car and looked around.

'I thought we were going to the pub? You just drove past it.'

'I know, but the car park'll be heaving on a Friday night so I thought it was easier to park at my house—well, actually my aunt's house. She's in a home and I'm caretaking it for her and trying to get it back into some sort of order. It's going to take me a while.'

'Yes, I think it might,' she murmured, eyeing the weeds that had taken over the gravel drive.

'I'll get there. Come on, my stomach's starting to make its presence felt.'

He ushered her across the road, and as they walked back towards the corner she could hear the hubbub of voices growing louder.

'Gosh, it's busy!' she said as they went in.

'It always is. I'll see if we can get a table, otherwise we might have to get them to cook for us and take it back to mine.' He leant on the bar and attracted the eye of a middle-aged woman. 'Hi, Maureen. Can you squeeze us in?'

'Oh, I think so. If you don't mind waiting a

minute, I've got a couple just about to leave. Here, have a menu and don't forget the specials board. Can I get you a drink while you wait?'

'I'm going to splash out and have tap water, but I'm driving. Iona? How about a glass of Prosecco to celebrate your first REBOA?'

'It was hardly mine.'

'Ah, well, that's just splitting hairs. Prosecco? Or gin and tonic? They have some interesting gins. And tonics.'

She wrestled with her common sense, and it lost. She smiled at him. 'A small glass of Prosecco would be lovely. Thank you.'

'And some bread, Maureen, please, before I keel over.'

'Poor baby,' Maureen said with a motherly but mildly mocking smile, and handed them their drinks before she disappeared into the kitchen.

'So, the menu. The twice baked Cromer crab soufflé with crayfish cream is fabulous. It's a starter but it makes a great main with one of the vegetable sides.'

'Is that what you're having?'

'No. I'm having the beer-battered fish and chips, because it's absolutely massive and I'm starving.' He grinned wickedly, and it made him look like a naughty boy. A very grown-up naughty boy. Her pulse did a little hiccup.

Maureen put the bread down in front of him. 'Is that your order, Joe? Fish and chips and mushy peas?'

'Please. Iona?'

'I'll go with the crab soufflé, please. It sounds lovely.'

'Have sweet potato fries,' he suggested. 'They're amazing.'

'I don't suppose they've got a single calorie in them, either,' she said, laughing.

'Calorie? No. Ridiculous idea. They do great puds, as well,' he added with another mischievous grin, and sank his teeth into a slice of fresh, warm baguette slathered with butter.

She couldn't help but smile.

CHAPTER TWO

'Wow. That was so tasty.'

'Mmm. And positively good for you.'

She used the last sweet potato fry to mop up the remains of the crayfish cream. 'Really?' she said sceptically.

He laughed and speared a fat, juicy flake of fish. 'I doubt it, but one can live in hope. So, what *were* you doing at the speed dating gig?' he asked, and she frowned, hugely reluctant to go back to that and wondering why she'd opened her mouth and blurted it out.

'I told you.'

His eyes widened, the fish on his fork frozen in mid-air. 'You were serious? I thought you were winding me up.'

'No. You probably deserved it, but I wasn't.'

He laughed, then looked back at her, those incredible eyes searching hers thoughtfully. 'You're genuinely serious, aren't you?'

'Yes. I genuinely am, but it's not why I was there, not really. I was helping set it up, and they talked me into taking a table, but a bit of me was wondering if anyone appropriate might rock up.'

'Iona.' His voice dropped, becoming quieter but somehow urgent and his eyes were suddenly deadly serious. 'Sorry, I know it's really none of my business—'

'No, it isn't, and I don't think this is really the time or the place.'

He frowned, nodded and let it go, but only with obvious reluctance. 'Yeah, you're right. OK. So—tell me about yourself. Apart from that.'

No way. 'I'd rather talk about you,' she said, smiling to soften it. 'What brings you to Yoxburgh?'

'Oh, that's easy. As I said, my aunt lives here in a home and I spent a lot of time here as a child, the hospital has an expanding IR department, they were looking for a specialist registrar, I wanted to broaden my experience and it seemed like a perfect fit. Plus I get a free house to live in,' he added with a little quirk of his lips that drew her attention back to them.

She wondered what it would be like to kiss them...

'So, why are you here?' he asked, and she hauled her mind back into order and edited her answer because the truth was too messy.

'Oh—similar reasons, really, work-wise. They've got a great ED department, I was looking for my first registrar's job, I'd worked in Bristol up to now but frankly I'd seen enough of it—' That was putting it mildly, but she wasn't going into that. 'And my family are based in Norfolk so it's not too far from them, and it's a great hospital, and I love the seaside. Not that I've seen much of it because the summer's been rubbish and, anyway, my shift pattern's pretty crazy and I haven't had a lot of time because I've been studying, too.'

'All work and no play, eh? Don't do that, Iona. Keep your work/life balance. It's really important.'

She tilted her head slightly and searched his eyes, because there'd been something in his voice...

'That sounded like personal experience,' she said, and his eyes changed again.

'Yeah, kind of. I know what it's like. My shift pattern's crazy, too, and on top of that I've got a mass of courses and exams coming up in the next year, but that's IR for you. It doesn't matter how hard I work, how much I learn, there'll always be more.'

'Is that "Do as I say, not as I do"?' she asked, and he laughed and nodded.

'Pretty much. Work can easily take over—not that I'm the best person to tell anybody how to run their life since I seem to have trashed my own, but there you go. You could always learn from my experience,' he said, and went back to his fish and chips.

'They look tasty. Can I pinch a chip?'

'Be my guest,' he said, and she took the last one off the plate as a shadow fell over the table.

'Was everything OK for you both?'

'Great, thanks.' He looked up at Maureen and smiled. 'Filling. I've eaten myself to a standstill.'

'So you don't want dessert? That's not like you.'

'Not tonight, I don't think. Iona?'

She would have loved a dessert. She'd spotted

one on the specials board, but Joe didn't seem inclined.

'I don't suppose you'd like to share the baked chocolate fondant?' she asked wistfully, and he just groaned and laughed.

'There's my resolve going down the drain.'

'That's a yes, then,' Maureen said with a smile. 'One, or two? And do you want coffee with it?'

He shook his head. 'Just one, and no coffee for me, Maureen. Iona?'

'No, I'm fine, thanks. The fondant will be more than enough.'

It took ten minutes to come, but it was worth the wait and she was enjoying the view and the company.

Maureen put the plate down between them, they picked up their spoons and Iona waited for him to cut it in half, but he didn't, just dug his spoon in, so she joined in and kept eating until their spoons clashed in the middle.

She glanced up, their eyes locked and he smiled and put his spoon down. 'Go on. Finish it. It was your idea.'

She didn't argue, just pulled the plate closer,

scraped it clean and put the spoon down a little sadly.

'That was delicious. All of it. Thank you.'

'You're welcome. Shall we go?'

She nodded, and he got to his feet, dropped a pile of notes on the bar in front of Maureen and they headed out into the darkness and a light drizzle.

'Oh. I didn't know it was going to do that,' she said with a rueful laugh, but he just reached out and took her hand in a firm, warm grip and they ran, guided by the light of his phone, and got back to the house before they were more than slightly damp.

'Coffee?' he asked, heading for the porch and standing under the shelter.

She hesitated on the drive. 'I thought you didn't want coffee?'

'No, I didn't want coffee *there*. I prefer mine, but I can't say that to Maureen, can I? It would break her heart.'

It made her laugh, as it was meant to, and she suddenly realised she did want a coffee, and she was also curious about the house, and his aunt, and—well, him, really.

And she was getting wet.

She stepped under the shelter of the porch and smiled. 'Coffee would be lovely. Thank you.'

He put the key in the door, turned it and pushed it open, flicking a switch that flooded the hall with light.

'Welcome to the seventies,' he said wryly, and stepped back to let her in.

It was stunning, and completely unexpected.

The walls were a pale acid green, but that wasn't what caught her eye, it was the way the ceiling sloped steeply up from right to left, rising along the line of the stairs and over the landing, creating a wonderful, open vaulted entrance hall.

'Wow! I love this!'

'Me, too. It goes downhill a bit from now on, mind,' he said with a low chuckle that did something odd to her insides. 'Come into the kitchen, I'll make you a coffee.'

She followed him through a glass door into a large rectangular room that ran away to the right across the back of the house. To the left were double doors into another room, in front of her beyond a large dining table was a set of bi-fold doors, opening she assumed to the garden, and on her right at the far end of the room was the kitchen area.

Not that there was much kitchen.

'Ahh. I see what you mean.'

He chuckled again. 'Yeah. It's a mess. I got the bi-folds put in and the dividing wall taken out, so I lost most of the units, but to be honest I haven't got the time or energy to decide what I want in here and it's a big job, starting with taking the floor up and re-screeding it because they weren't quite level. So I'm learning to love the tiny scraps of seventies worktop and the ridiculously huge sink and the utter lack of storage, but it's only me so it's fine. And the pub's handy when I get desperate,' he added with a grin. 'So, coffee. Caf, decaf, black, white, frothy?'

She stared at him, slightly mesmerised by the sight of him propped against the sink with his arms folded, relaxed and at ease. It was gradually dawning on her just how incredibly attractive he was, how well put together, how confident, caring, thoughtful, sexy—

'Hello?'

She pulled herself together and tried to smile.

'Sorry. I was just a bit stunned by the kitchen,' she lied. 'Um—can you do a decaf frothy?'

'Sure, that's what I'm having.' He flipped a capsule into the machine, put a mug under the spout and pressed a button, put milk into the frother and then propped himself up again and frowned thoughtfully at her.

'What?'

'Nothing. Well, nothing you want to hear. You told me to butt out.'

'Are we back to that?' she said with a sigh.

'Yes, we are, because... Iona, if you want a baby, why wouldn't you look for a partner?'

'I've tried that,' she said, really not wanting to go there. 'And, anyway, that's not what it's about.'

He looked puzzled, then shrugged. 'OK, so why not go through a proper sperm bank or clinic? The risks to you are *huge* if you don't use a donor regulated by the Human Fertilisation and Embryology Authority. They won't have had genetic testing, no sperm quality check—it's a minefield, even if you don't take into account the risk of picking up a life-changing infection such as Hepatitis or HIV. The screening process is so thorough, so intensive, the physical and mental health screening, sperm quality, family medical history, motivation—and the children have the right to trace their fathers now once they're eighteen, so nobody's going to be doing it for anything other than the right reasons. Why on earth would you go anywhere else?'

'I wouldn't. I haven't. I'm not that stupid, so you can relax and stop fretting. I wasn't serious about picking up a random stranger, I was winding you up, really, but I am looking for a sperm donor. That much was true.' She studied him thoughtfully. 'You seem to know an awful lot about it,' she added, searching his eyes, and something in them changed again.

He looked away briefly, then back, the silence between them somehow deafening in the quiet room.

'Yeah. I do,' he said finally, as if it had been dragged out of him. 'I've done it, but that was years ago, before I properly understood the knock-on effect of it.'

Wow. 'Knock-on effect?' she asked, still processing the fact that he'd been a donor. Ironic, since she'd mentally given him ten out of ten, but he didn't need to know that.

'Yes. Wondering—you know—about the children, if there are any, if they're OK? That sort of stuff.'

'Can they contact you?'

'No, because I did it before the law changed, but I can still provide contact details if I want to via the HFEA, and I could also find out how many children there are, their ages, their genders, but I can't contact them to find out if they're OK, and that troubles me. Are they happy? Are they safe? What are their parents like? Are they still together? Are they well? I just don't know, and it's unlikely I ever will, and it bugs me.'

'But it's not your worry, surely?'

'Yes, it is,' he said emphatically. 'I know they aren't technically my children, but in a way they are because without me they wouldn't exist, so morally I feel responsible. What if they're unhappy? What if someone's hurting them? It's unlikely, I know that, but still I worry. Of course I worry.'

'But as you said, it's highly unlikely and, anyway, you've signed over that right, that responsibility. They're not your children, any more than this would be my child. I'm doing it for my sister, and I won't have any rights, I know that because I'll sign them all over to Isla and Steve when they adopt it, but I'm fine with that. That's why I'm doing it, not because I want a child.'

His eyes widened and his jaw dropped a fraction. 'You're going to *give it away*?' he said. 'Iona, that's— Will you be able to do that? It's going to take so much courage. What if you change your mind when it comes to it? Are you able to change your mind?'

Her heart gave a little hiccup, but she ignored it. 'I won't change my mind, because there's no room in my life for a child now, and I don't know if there ever will be, and this is something I can do for Isla and Steve, and I want to help them because I love them.'

'Yes, of course you do, but—' He rammed a hand through his hair, his eyes troubled. 'I only gave away my DNA and that feels hard enough sometimes. You're talking about cradling your own baby inside your body for *nine months*! How will you be able to give it away, even if it is to your sister? I know you love her and you know her very well, so you know the baby will be safe and loved, but—what about *you*, Iona? How will *you* feel? And what if they split up? What if their marriage breaks down?'

'It won't! And this is my sister, Joe—my *identical twin* sister, so genetically it would be identical to a child of her own. It could *be* her own. It'll be just like being the incubator for their own baby, and I want to do it for her because I love her and I want to help her—'

'I know you do, but...?'

'But? How many siblings do you have?'

'None.'

'None?' She laughed disbelievingly. 'None. So how can you *possibly* judge my motives?'

'I can't. I'm not judging your motives, I wouldn't presume to do that and I'm sure you're doing it for the all right reasons. I have immense respect for your courage in even contemplating it. I'm only thinking of the impact it would have on you, knowing how hard it's been for me, and what I've done is *nothing* compared to what you're talking about. Please tell me you've thought it through.'

'I thought you were making me a coffee?' she

said, changing the subject abruptly, and he swore softly, threw away the one he'd made ages ago and dropped another capsule in the machine. Then he scrubbed a hand through his hair again and sighed as he turned back to her.

'Sorry.'

'Are you?'

He sighed again. 'Yes and no. I know I keep banging the same old drum, Iona, but I'm really worried about you now.'

'You really don't need to be, Joe, I do know what I'm doing. It's not an idle thought. I've researched it, I've considered it at length, dis-cussed it endlessly—I'm not stupid.'

'I never said you were. Just maybe too kind for your own good. Whose idea was it?'

'Mine. All mine.'

'And they said yes?'

She rolled her eyes. 'Yes, they said yes, but not until they'd tried to talk me out of it, but I could tell they didn't really want to do that, they just wanted to be sure that I was sure, and I am.'

'Have you ever been pregnant?'

She shook her head, feeling a pang of regret

because they'd tried and failed. 'No. Have you?' she asked, and he laughed.

'I don't believe so.'

'Then how can you lecture me on what it'll feel like?'

'Because I have imagination? Because I have empathy? Because I know how hard I've found even doing what I did?'

'But it's different to your situation. I *know* who the baby's going to, and I know it'll be loved and cherished and brought up with my values. Did you have any control over who had your sperm?'

He shook his head. 'No. And that's at the root of my worries, I have to admit, because I can never be utterly sure my ch—' He cut himself off. 'My *offspring* will be loved and cared for as I would have loved and cared for them.'

She searched his eyes—those gorgeous, penetrating, honest eyes—and she could read them clearly, could see the genuine worry he felt for his unknown children, the responsibility he felt for their happiness over which he had no control.

'You're a good man, do you know that?' she said softly, and he laughed and turned away, making a production of spooning out the froth onto her new coffee.

'Chocolate sprinkles?'

'Is it powder?'

'No, it's flakes of real chocolate.'

'Oh, yes, please. I love those.'

'Me, too. Here.'

He handed it to her, and she went up on tiptoe and brushed a kiss against his cheek.

'Thank you.'

He looked slightly startled. 'It's only a coffee.'

'It's not for the coffee, it's for caring—about the children you don't know, about me—just—for caring.'

He hesitated, staring down into her eyes, and then he gave a fleeting smile.

'You're welcome. I didn't mean to interfere, but I can't stand by and watch a friend sleep-walk into potential unhappiness without saying anything.'

'Am I a friend?' she asked, and he gave her a thoughtful half-smile.

'I think you could be. I'm not in the habit of spilling my guts to people who aren't.'

He turned back to the coffee maker, and she

perched on a chair at the big old table, a funny warm feeling inside, and watched him make his own coffee, his movements as deft and sure as they'd been in Resus. He rinsed out the milk frother, sat down opposite her and met her eyes.

'Talking about spilling my guts, it's a bit late to worry about this, but you're the only person outside my family who I've ever told about any of this stuff, so I'd be grateful if you'd keep it to yourself.'

She nodded, surprised that he'd even felt he had to ask her. 'Of course I will. I'm amazed you told me. It's not the sort of thing people talk about—and snap, by the way. Only my sister and brother-in-law know. We haven't even told the rest of the family.'

'Yes, I can understand that.' He gave a wry chuckle. 'I didn't mean to tell you, by the way, it just sort of came out, but—Iona, please be careful, and if you do decide to do it, do it properly? Don't go and have some unpremeditated random one-night stand with someone just because they're tall and blond and have good bone structure.'

That made her laugh. 'I was sort of joking, but

it's what my brother-in-law looks like, and we've been trying to find a sperm donor who at least has some of his physical characteristics. They tried IVF and got a few live embryos, but the quality wasn't great and none of them implanted, although nobody could say why for certain. Steve's sperm quality isn't good, so she's tried AI with a tall, blue-eyed blond donor, which didn't work, and I've tried AI three times with Steve's semen and not got pregnant.'

A little frown appeared fleetingly between his brows. 'I didn't realise you'd got that far down the line,' he said slowly.

'Oh, yes. This isn't a spur-of-the-moment thing, Joe. We've been talking about it for ages. That's part of the reason I took this job, to be nearer to them. So, anyway, it needs to be another sperm donor since the one she tried has reached his limit of donations, and we can't find another one that ticks all the boxes on any of the donor sites, at least not the physical appearance boxes. And, yes, I know that's the least important thing in a way, but it's tough enough for them without the child looking like a cuckoo in the nest. Maybe I need to go on a cruise up the fjords and try and find a Viking,' she added lightly, winding him up again, and he spluttered into his coffee and wiped the froth off his lip, his eyes brimming with laughter.

'Do you know who goes on fjord cruises? Tourists, Iona. People like my parents. And, believe me, they don't look like Vikings.'

'Oh, well, there goes that idea, then.' She laughed, then sat back, cradling her coffee. 'Tell me about them—your parents.'

'My parents? What can I tell you? My dad's called Bill, my mother's Mary, they're in their late sixties. Dad's an ex-army officer, invalided out after an explosives accident that left him with—well, let's call them life-changing injuries, for want of a better description. And as if that wasn't enough, my mother, who was pregnant at the time, lost her baby.'

'Oh, Joe, that's awful. That's so sad.'

He nodded. 'They think it was probably the shock of the severity of his injuries that caused her miscarriage. It might have been, or it might not, but because of his injuries it was their last chance and they lost it. Hence why I'm an only child. And despite his best efforts to get rid of her, my mother's stuck by him and they have a great relationship, but underlying it all is this sadness, a sort of grief I guess for the baby they lost and the children they never had.'

'Hence why you were a sperm donor,' she said slowly, understanding him now at last. 'To help people like them.'

'Yes. Or at least partly. I was four when the accident happened, and I spent a lot of that year living with my aunt and uncle here, and it was the nearest they got to having their own children and we're still really close. Elizabeth, my aunt, is my father's much older sister, and she's widowed now, but she and her husband built this house in their thirties as their family home, and the family never happened. She's never got over that.'

'Does she know what you've done?'

'Oh, yes. She was the first person I told and she's been hugely supportive.' He smiled fondly. 'Oddly, I can talk to her about things I could never tell my parents.'

'I don't think that's odd. I feel the same. There are things I can tell my aunt I'd never tell my mother.' She looked up at him again, watching his face carefully as she spoke because she'd just had a crazy idea and she didn't know how it was going to land.

'Talking of families—are you busy this weekend?'

'Why?' he asked warily, turning his head slightly to the side and eyeing her suspiciously.

'Because I need a plus one. My baby brother's getting married tomorrow, and I have to go to his wedding, and I really, really don't want to go on my own.'

He frowned. 'Are you suggesting I should come with you? Because there's no way in hell I'm going to another wedding as long as I live, not after my catastrophic car crash of a marriage.'

She laughed wryly, even though it wasn't funny. 'I can understand that. It's exactly why I don't want to go, except I never got to the altar. I found out three days before my wedding that he'd slept with the stripper on his stag weekend, and when I challenged him he said something about it just being drunken high spirits, so when I asked him if he'd still been drunk on the subsequent four occasions he started grovelling, but I'd had enough so I called it off, and then he went round slagging me off to all our friends, saying I'd dumped him without hearing his side of it.'

'What *side*? It sounds to me like you're well off out of it.'

'Oh, tell me about it, but I still don't want to go to Johnnie's wedding on my own with all the friends and relatives who would have been at mine, who'll feel morally obliged to come and tell me how sorry they were and try and get all the juicy details. Especially not since it's also the same church I should have got married in less than two years ago.'

'Where is it?' he asked, surprising her.

'Where? Norfolk. A village just west of Norwich, not all that different to this one, but at least it's a nice, easy drive.'

He grunted. 'It's not the drive I have issues with, it's the wedding. Watching someone making their vows and wondering if they have the *slightest* idea what they've let themselves in for.'

'What, like your parents, who by the sound of it are devoted to each other? Or your uncle and aunt?'

He gave a sharp sigh. 'They're different.'

'No, they're not. They sound like my sister and

brother-in-law, and my parents, and my uncle and aunt. And Johnnie and Kate love each other to bits. They always have. They're childhood sweethearts, and they're wonderful together, but I just know I'm going to cry and make an idiot of myself and everybody'll think it's because of...'

'So you want me there to—what? Pass you tissues?'

She laughed at that, at the thought of him handing her tissues like a production line as she sobbed her way through the ceremony that she'd been denied.

'Well, I think you need to do something fairly mega to make up for being arrogant and then stealing my stethoscope. Is it really too much to ask?'

She was only joking, never for a moment thinking he'd agree, not now she knew he'd had an apparently disastrous marriage, and he stared at her slightly open-mouthed for a moment.

'I didn't *steal* it. I just forgot to give it back.'

'So you're not denying you were arrogant?' she said with a little coaxing smile, and to her surprise he groaned and rolled his eyes. Was he weakening?

'I'm not staying over,' he said, jabbing his finger at her to add emphasis to every word. 'I don't want to stay over.'

So he'd go? 'Nor do I, but it goes on until midnight so it's a bit late to drive back. I should be there now, as well, but I lied and told them I was on call.'

He gave her an odd look. 'Why would you do that?'

'To get out of the family dinner, so they didn't have to tiptoe round the elephant in the room? But I don't really have a choice about tomorrow night. They'll be expecting me to stay, and I'm sure there'll be room for you somewhere. You can have my room if it comes to that. And you'd get to meet my sister and brother-in-law, too, and see why I want to make them happy.'

She left it there, hanging, holding her breath, and he said nothing for an age, just stared into his coffee, swirling it round and watching the froth, then he lifted it to his mouth, drained it and put it down with exaggerated care.

'OK. I'll do it,' he said, his eyes deadly serious now. 'As much as anything so I can meet them, and find out what kind of people would let you do this for them, because they'd have to be pretty special for you to make that kind of sacrifice.'

She felt her eyes fill and grabbed his hand, squeezing it hard. 'They are—and thank you! You're a life-saver.'

'Don't bother to thank me. I'll probably spend most of the journey there and back trying to talk sense into you. So, what's the dress code, and when do we need to leave?'

He picked her up at eleven, and she took one look at him in a blinding white dress shirt, black bow tie and immaculately cut black dress trousers, and felt her heart rate pick up.

He took her bag, put it in the back of the car and held the door for her, then slid behind the wheel and clipped on his seat belt, drawing her attention to his hands. He had beautiful hands. Clever hands.

'OK?'

'Yes. You scrub up quite nicely,' she said rashly, and he turned his head and met her eyes.

'You don't do too badly yourself,' he said, and then turned away before she could analyse the expression in them, but he'd looked…

'What's the postcode?' he asked, and he keyed it into his satnav, started the engine and pulled away.

She swallowed, fastened her seat belt and took a deep breath, and he turned the radio on, saving her from the need to break the silence.

'So, why interventional radiology?' she asked after an hour interspersed with the odd comment about landmarks and idle chat.

He gave her a wry look and laughed as he turned his attention back to the road. 'Are you afraid I'll start lecturing you again or something?'

She felt her mouth twitch. 'No, I'm not. I doubt if I could stop you, anyway, you're like a dog with a bone. I'm just genuinely curious. It's seems a bit...'

'Dry?' he offered.

'Exactly. Or maybe not, not after what I saw you do yesterday.'

He laughed again. 'Oh, that was pure theatre. Most of it's much more mundane and measured. And the amount of learning, the sheer volume of what you have to know, is staggering. There are so many uses for it, so many different conditions that can be cured or alleviated by what is essentially a very minimal intervention. Every part of the body has a blood supply, and by using the blood vessels we can deliver life-saving interventions directly where they're needed—stents, cancer treatments, clearing blockages, making blockages to stop bleeding—it's endless.

'We used to think that keyhole surgery was the holy grail, but IR is expanding so fast and there are so many potential uses for it it's mind-boggling. I spend most of my waking hours either practising it or studying it, because if I don't, I won't know enough and I'll make an error and someone will suffer when it could have been avoided.'

'Is that what went wrong with your marriage?' she asked without thinking, and he flashed her a glance.

'What, that it suffered because I didn't study it enough?' he asked drily, and she laughed.

'No, I meant you being a workaholic, but that wouldn't have helped, either.'

He gave a soft snort, and nodded. 'Probably not. No, she fancied the idea of being a doctor's wife—the money, the social status—she had no idea what being married to a junior hospital doctor actually meant.'

'She can't have been that clueless.'

'Oh, she wasn't—far from it. She just hated her job and thought I'd be a good meal ticket, but then she realised that it wasn't just for a year or two, it was going to be like it for at least a decade, and so...'

'So?'

'She found a way to deal with it. I didn't know about it, but I knew she was unhappy, and one day I thought, To hell with it, I won't stay at work practising in the skills lab, I'll go home, take her out for dinner. And I caught her in bed—*our* bed—with her lover.'

She sucked in a breath. 'Oh, Joe, that's awful.'

His hands tightened on the wheel. 'Yeah, tell me about it. He wasn't the first, either, apparently, but it was my fault as much as hers. I was neglecting her, I was constantly tired, we hardly had a social life to speak of—it was no wonder, really, that she'd got bored with waiting for me to notice her and turned to other men.'

'You still don't do it like that,' she said, furious on his behalf. 'You stay, or you leave. You don't cheat.'

'Exactly, and especially not as many times as she told me she had, or for as long. So I left. And then, even though technically she was the one in the wrong, she got half the equity from the house. And we lived in London, so she did very nicely out of it because I'd bought it two years before I met her and pushed myself to the limit, and by the time the divorce settlement was through I'd been priced out of the market.'

She reached out and laid her hand lightly over his on the steering wheel. 'I'm sorry, Joe.'

His head turned and his mouth flickered into a wry smile. 'Don't be sorry. It was a lesson learned. I won't make the same mistake again.'

He drew in a slow breath, let it out on a huff and smiled again. 'So, tell me about your family so I don't put my foot in it.'

'Oh, there's not much to tell. My father's an accountant, my mother was a nurse, my sister's a town planner, her husband's an architect, my brother's a solicitor and Kate, his fiancée, is a legal executive. We're all boring normal, except that Isla and Steve can't seem to make a baby, and to put the cherry on top, Kate's just found out she's pregnant.'

'Ouch.'

'Yes. Ouch. And ignore your satnav, you need to turn left here.'

CHAPTER THREE

'YOU DIDN'T CRY. There I was, with tissues at the ready—'

'Oh, I nearly did, but only for the right reasons, and it was a lovely wedding.'

He laughed softly. 'I suppose it was, as weddings go.'

They were sitting at one of the round tables in the marquee that had housed the reception, alone now because the others had gone off to mingle, and he absently unwrapped another of the heart-shaped chocolates covered in red foil and offered it to her.

She reached over and took it out of his fingers and put it in her mouth. 'Thank you for coming with me. I know you didn't want to.'

He unwrapped another chocolate, balled up the foil and flicked it idly into the middle of the table. 'No, I didn't, but hey. We've survived, and the band's starting up, judging by the sound of it. Fancy a dance?'

'Really? You want to dance?'

'Not really, I'd rather sit here and eat chocolates, but if it'll keep you out of mischief and stop you crawling off into the bushes with the best man, then I guess I probably should.'

'Why would I do that?' she asked, half laughing, half shocked, and he just rolled his eyes and smiled.

'I was joking—but he is tall and blond and vaguely Nordic.'

'And happily married to a very pregnant woman, in case you hadn't noticed. Anyway, I wouldn't do that!'

'Good. One less thing for me to worry about,' he teased.

Iona stood up, wobbled slightly and grabbed his hand, hauling him to his feet. 'You're very rude. I'm beginning to regret inviting you. Come on, Johnnie and Kate are going to have the first dance, and then, since you're so keen, you can dance with me, but you'd better not tread on my toes.'

'I wouldn't dream of it.' He looked down into

her eyes, soft and almost luminous, touched with stardust from the thousands of tiny fairy lights strung around the marquee, and had a sudden, burning urge to kiss her.

Which he was *not going to do.*

Then she took a step and saved herself by grabbing him. 'Oh, these stupid shoes. I knew they were too high, they keep catching on the matting.'

She kicked them off under the table, and he slung an arm round her waist, steered her to the dance floor and then endured watching her loved-up brother and his new bride dancing a shamelessly sentimental waltz. Then it was over, and Iona stepped onto the dance floor and started to move, and his heart revved up a gear.

Oh, this was not good. His tongue glued itself to the roof of his mouth, his body roared to life and he kicked himself for agreeing to come with her. Because she was incredibly sexy, in a quietly sensual way that he hadn't really registered before, and he wanted her. Right here, right now. She moved with sinuous grace, her body seeming to flow as she swayed to the beat of the music, and when she reached out and grabbed his hands and drew him in he didn't know whether to laugh or cry.

Or kiss her...

But in the end he did none of them, he just danced, and to his surprise he enjoyed it, despite the cheesy wedding music and the spotlight that was circulating round the dancers and picking the couples out one by one. Including them, of course, and she played up to it, twirling and twisting like a candle flame, her face alight with laughter as she whirled into his arms and kissed him.

For show, to prove to everyone that she was so over her feckless ex? Either that or she was tipsy, and he didn't think she was. Not that he would have blamed her, he would have been in her shoes, but then the light moved on and she was still pressed against him, her body warm and soft and lithe, tantalising him.

Not good. He still wanted to kiss her—*needed* to kiss her, properly this time and definitely not in public—but then to his relief the band launched into 'YMCA' and she straightened up and started to sing along with everyone else, trying and failing to get the actions right.

'You're hopeless,' he said, laughing at her, and spent the next few minutes face to face with her, reminding her of the actions and singing at the top of his voice along with all the others. Not that he wanted to, but it knocked spots off watching her with his tongue hanging out and his libido running riot.

He was a good dancer. An amazing dancer, actually. And you could tell a lot about what kind of lover a man was by the way he danced.

And she couldn't believe she was thinking that.

'Come on,' she said, grabbing his hand and towing him off the dance floor before she did something inappropriate. 'I need air and water. Or maybe coffee.'

They went back to their table, she recovered her shoes and took one step before she kicked them off again.

'Right, grab that bottle of wine off the table and follow me,' she said, scooping up the shoes and a handful of the chocolate hearts that still littered the table.

He followed her out of the marquee and into the house via the front door, and she threw her shoes onto the stairs and headed down the hall to the kitchen.

'Are you all right with dogs?' she asked over her shoulder, but it was too late to worry because the dogs had sneaked past her and were already mugging him.

'Hello, dogs, did you think you'd been forgotten?' he said softly, and to her amazement he was fondling their ears and rubbing their tummies.

'Come on, you two hussies, back in here.' She ushered them all—him and the dogs—into the kitchen, filled the kettle and put it on, then plonked herself down at the kitchen table and put her feet up on the edge. 'I hate those shoes,' she grumbled, inspecting her feet, and she heard a dry chuckle from Joe.

'What? Why are you laughing?'

'Well, it isn't rocket science to know that putting your feet into instruments of torture is going to hurt. Is there any chance of a proper coffee?' he asked, dumping his jacket and undoing his bow tie.

How could he possibly look even sexier?

'A proper coffee?' she croaked.

'Yeah, as in a mug, rather than a delicate little bone china thimble? I'm guessing it's going to be a long night.'

'Oh, I don't doubt it, but Kate and Johnnie aren't leaving, they're staying here, so we can quit when we like. I need to find out where we're sleeping, though— Ah, Mum. Perfect timing. Can we find a bed for Joe, please?'

'Not until I get these shoes off.' Her mother plonked herself down and winced. 'Ooh, that's better. Right. Bedrooms. I've put you in the little single room, darling, I hope you don't mind, because Kate's parents are in your room. Mike, where are we going to put Joe? The study?'

'Could do. It's got the sofa bed. It's that or in here with the dogs unless you want to bunk up with Iona. Oh, well done, you picked up some of the chocolates. I'm Mike, by the way, Iona's father. I don't think we've been properly introduced.'

Joe got to his feet and shook hands. 'Joe Baker. I'm a colleague of Iona's.'

Her father searched his eyes. 'Just a colleague? That's a shame.'

'Dad! Joe, I'm so sorry, just ignore him.'

But Joe was laughing, and he sent her a tiny, almost unnoticeable wink as he sat down again.

'So, what do you do?' her father asked, like a dog with a bone. 'Are you in the ED with Iona?'

'No. No, we have worked together,' he said, stretching the point so far she nearly laughed out loud, 'but I'm an interventional radiologist.'

'What in the heck is that?' her father asked, and so Joe blessedly launched into a long-winded explanation that kept them all neatly off the subject of how long they'd known each other and exactly what their relationship was.

She could have kissed him. Maybe it was just as well she really, really couldn't…

They left the following morning after an early brunch, and as they drove away she rested her head back with a sigh and shut her eyes.

He glanced across at her. She looked tired. Maybe she needed to go home to bed.

With him? He felt his mouth tip into a rueful smile. No. Too soon—although it didn't feel it, not after dancing with her last night…

'Hangover?' he asked, glancing across at her again, and she shook her head.

'No, just a relieved-it's-all-over-over. And, actually, it wasn't nearly as bad as it could have been.' She rolled her head towards him and rested a hand lightly on his shoulder. 'Thank you so much for doing this, Joe. I know it can't have been easy, but it made so much difference to me having you there. It just deflected all that sympathy I was expecting, so thank you.'

'You're welcome,' he said, and realised he meant it. 'As you said, it wasn't as bad as it could have been, and some of it was quite fun. So how come it was at your parents' house and not Kate's parents'?'

'They live abroad, so it was easier and cheaper to do it here. They all split the cost, I think, and let's face it, it had already been planned for me so they all knew what was involved and it made it fairly simple. They all liked you, by the way. My father's desperately match-making, and Isla even asked how well I knew you and if there was any way I could persuade you to be the sperm donor.'

What? 'Tell me you didn't tell her?'

'Well, no, of course I didn't. I promised I wouldn't. I don't think she was serious, but I put her off, anyway. I told her there was no way I could ask you, I didn't know you nearly well enough, and she said that was a shame because you'd be perfect. Which you're not, because A, you don't want to do it, and, B, you don't look like a Viking.'

All of which sounded reasonably plausible, but he had still a gut feeling he'd been played. Thank God he hadn't given in to his instincts and found a way to sleep with her last night.

'So why on earth would she ask? I thought the Viking thing was set in stone?'

'No, not any more, apparently. Since the law changed there are far fewer donors, so they've realised that they have to compromise because other things are much more important. And, anyway, the baby stands a fair chance of looking like me and Isla, so it's not really that big an issue.'

'So is this why you really asked me to the wedding?' he asked bluntly. 'So she could size me up as a sperm donor now they've changed their criteria?'

She stared at him open-mouthed. 'No! Absolutely not! It hadn't even *occurred* to me to ask you. Well, no, that's not strictly true, it *had* occurred to me, but that was before you told me how you felt about it and I realised it would be pointless asking you anyway, so I dismissed it. I certainly didn't ask you to the wedding with that in mind, because apart from anything else she's only just told me about their changed priorities. I just wanted someone with me to deflect all the sympathy, and it was a way for you to meet them and realise how nice they are so you could maybe understand why I want to do it, and get off my case a bit.'

'They are nice,' he agreed, still not quite convinced of her motive for inviting him. 'They're lovely. I'm sure they'll be great parents. But it doesn't change how I feel, Iona—either about me doing it again, which I never will so please *don't* ask me, or about what it'll do to you to give up your child, which you can't know until the time comes. And it doesn't matter how worthy the intended parents might be, that's irrelevant to me because I'm not worried about them, I'm worried about you. I have huge sympathy for their situation, but you're my concern, not them.'

'I realise that, but they are mine, and it's in my

power to make them happy, and I don't see why I shouldn't do that—and, anyway, when did I ask you to worry about me?'

'You haven't—'

'No, I haven't. And how you could even *think* I'd trick you into coming to the wedding so they could assess your donor potential, for goodness' sake? I'd *never* do that without discussing it with you first. It just shows how little you know about me if you think I could possibly be that devious. I wish I'd never told you…'

She turned her face away and he let his breath out on a long, quiet sigh, pulled over into a handy layby behind a lorry and switched off the engine.

The driver got out and walked past them, heading no doubt for the tea hut behind them, and Joe reached for her with a sigh.

'Come here.'

'Why?' she asked, her voice choked.

'So I can give you a hug,' he said, his voice softer now, but she shrugged off his hands and he dropped them back in his lap with another sigh. 'I'm sorry. I didn't mean to upset you, it was just a knee-jerk reaction, and you're right, I don't really know you, Iona, but it doesn't stop me caring deeply about what happens to you or worrying that you're going to do something that could hurt you so badly. I just didn't want you sleepwalking into it.'

'I know, you keep saying that,' she said, her voice sounding clogged with tears, 'but you don't have to worry about me. I'm a big girl, Joe. I can do this. I don't need counselling, and certainly not from someone who doubts my motives about everything!'

She straightened up, swiping her cheeks with the backs of her hands, and he reached into his pocket and pulled out a tissue.

'Here.'

She took it with a little hiccupping laugh. 'You always knew you were going to end up doing this, didn't you?'

'Not like this. I'm sorry, I truly am. I don't want to fight with you, but I just had a horrible sinking feeling you might have engineered the whole situation.'

She looked up at him, yesterday's mascara smudging onto the fine skin beneath her wounded eyes. 'How could I have done that?

Even if I was that kind of person, how could I have done it? I only met you on Friday!'

'May I remind you that you told me in words of one syllable that you were on the look-out for a sperm donor, so it's not like it's a huge leap.'

She glared at him, her eyes red-rimmed and filled with disgust. 'I so shouldn't have told you. It's got nothing to do with you anyway, and just because you've been a sperm donor doesn't give you the right to tell me what to do, but trust me, if I'd seriously considered you or anyone else as a potential donor, I would have asked openly, not resorted to subterfuge.'

'So if it had been some other wedding and they were going to be there, you wouldn't have asked me to go with you?'

'No. Why would I? I wouldn't have needed you there, but it wasn't, it was Johnnie's wedding and I had to go, I had no choice. He's my baby brother, and with Kate pregnant and rubbing salt into the wound, I had to be there for Isla and Steve, too. And it was a chance for you to meet them.'

'Are you absolutely sure that wasn't my real role, even subconsciously? To be dangled in front of them to make them think there was some hope you'd found a suitable victim?' he asked, hating himself but feeling gutted at the same time that yet again, he might have been used, not for himself but for what he could offer. 'Because you seemed to me to be fine at the wedding, and I'm not convinced you needed my support at all.'

She glared at him, her face a riot of emotions, none of them good. 'Of course I did, I was hanging by a thread! For heaven's sake, listen to me, you're not hearing what I'm saying! You were just my plus one. No ulterior motive. And what do you mean, *victim*? You make me sound like a black widow spider—'

'OK, victim was a bad choice of word—'

'Tell me about it!'

'But if you knew you didn't want to go alone, why not ask someone else to go with you? You surely have friends you could have asked, and you must have known about it for months.'

'Of course I have, but I've been putting it out of my mind, refusing to face up to it, trying not to think about it. And suddenly it was Friday night and there it was, right in front of my nose, and I realised I couldn't do it. And then there you were, and I thought maybe, if I could twist your arm—'

'I don't buy it. It just all seems too convenient when you've only just met me and you're looking for—'

'How big *is* your ego? For the last time, Joe, I don't *want* your bloody sperm!' she yelled, and the truck driver on his way back to his cab jerked to a halt and slopped coffee on his hand, his mouth open.

'Well, that's me told,' he said mildly. 'Shall I wind the windows down so you can repeat it, just in case there was anyone else who didn't hear?'

'No! Just take me home,' she mumbled, sliding down into her seat, and he fired up the engine and dropped the window.

'Don't worry, mate, she wasn't talking to you,' he said grimly to the wary truck driver, and gunning the engine he pulled back out onto the road and shot her a glance.

She was staring straight ahead, her face a mask, and he turned the radio on and drove the rest of the way without another word, furious with himself for allowing her to dupe him. And to think he'd been contemplating taking her to bed!

But his thoughts were in turmoil, and by the time they'd reached Yoxburgh and he'd dropped her off and driven halfway home, he'd got his battered ego back in its box where it belonged and had the sickening realisation that he'd made a dreadful mistake, and that somewhere along the way he'd lost something infinitely precious that he hadn't even known he'd had.

He was on a course all week, he'd told her, so at least she'd be spared the agony of bumping into him again after that humiliating fiasco in the layby.

Not that it was all her fault, not at all. How could he possibly have thought she was that conniving? But he'd dropped her off, leaving the engine running as he'd lifted her bag out of the back, and she'd taken it from him and gone inside without a word, and now the next time she saw him it would be unbearably awkward.

She shouldn't have yelled at him like that, even if he'd deserved it, but she'd been so hurt, so distraught that he could have thought so little of her that she'd just lashed out.

Frankly she never wanted to speak to him again as long as she lived, but hospitals were too small to get away with that, and he'd already proved his worth in the ED so he was bound to be back. She had to clear the air, but how?

She didn't have his mobile number so she couldn't even text him. But she did know where he lived. She'd write a card and put it through his letterbox so he'd get it when he came back. Better late than never, and there was no way she wanted to bump into him in the hospital with a cloud like that hanging over them. She just hoped she could find his house in daylight— but not today. Not until he was out of the way because she wasn't sure she could trust herself not to say something awful.

As if she hadn't already.

Damn…

Damn.

Why had he said that? Any of it? Why had he believed even for a second that she could have tricked him into going to the wedding?

And she hadn't been all right. She'd been silent and withdrawn until they'd got to the church, then she'd plastered on a brave smile and dazzled him and everyone else. Except during the vows, and because they'd been packed closely together in the pews, he'd felt a shudder run through her when the priest had said the words, 'and forsaking all others'.

Not surprising, under the circumstances. The image of Natalie and her lover locked together on the tangled bedding was burned on his memory for all time.

It was all he'd been able to see for the rest of the service, so wrapped up in his own bitterness and regret he'd been oblivious to Iona. How had she taken it? She hadn't cried, he knew that, but he'd seen nothing of the inner turmoil that she'd undoubtedly been feeling. He'd been too preoccupied with his own.

He swore and pulled over to the side of the road. He had to go back, to do something to repair the damage he'd caused, because he had to leave shortly and head for Manchester for the course he was booked on, and then he'd have no way of contacting her until he was back.

He'd be gone for days, and he couldn't leave it that long without apologising. Not even he was that much of an egotistical bastard.

So he swung the car round, headed back and pulled up outside her house and rang the doorbell.

Nothing. Not a sound, not a flicker of movement through the frosted glass in the door—nothing. He rang it again, and then again, but she didn't come to the door, so he stepped back to the edge of the pavement and looked up, but there was no sign of her at the windows, and he had no idea where her flat was in the house.

He could leave her a note—except he had nothing with him to write with or on, so that wouldn't work. One last try?

No. If she was going to answer, she would have done it. He let out a heavy sigh, turned on his heel and went back to the car, slammed the door and rested his head on the steering wheel.

Idiot. Stupid, stupid idiot. How could he ever have considered that she'd use that kind of subterfuge? She couldn't lie to save her life, and when he'd asked her why she was at the speed-dating event, she'd told him the truth. Not the whole truth, not until later, but probably nothing but the truth.

It was him who'd brought up the sperm donor thing, him who'd taken her back to his house, given her coffee and spilled his guts about his marriage. Why, he had no idea. It was so unlike him he still couldn't understand why he'd done it, but there was just something about Iona that seemed to drag the truth out of him, whether he wanted it out or not.

Oh, well. She didn't want it now. Didn't want anything from him, if she wasn't answering the door. Maybe it was as well. He had things to do before he left, like more research into the topic of the course, and a quick visit to his aunt. And it wouldn't hurt to muck out the fridge and get rid of the things that were past their use-by date so the house didn't reek when he got home after the course.

Angry, dispirited and utterly disgusted at himself, he straightened up, reached for the key and saw her there, standing by the car with her arms wrapped defensively round her and her eyes red-rimmed and wary.

He got out, shut the car door and stood there in silence facing her. *What the hell had he done?*

'I don't know where to start,' he said eventually. 'There's nothing I can say to make it better, except to say I'm sorry. So sorry. You didn't deserve that. You didn't deserve any of it.'

Her arms tightened round her waist but her eyes didn't leave his. 'No, I didn't. She did a real number on you, didn't she? Your ex?'

'Yes.' He nodded slowly. 'Yes, she did. But you know what? I'm a grown man, I shouldn't be letting the actions of someone in the past affect the way I interact with people now, but sometimes I think I can't trust my own judgement, and then if I think I've been lied to I lash out, but I shouldn't have done that, I shouldn't have said the things I said and hurt you like that. I never meant to, and if I'd stopped to think about it for a second, I would have known you weren't lying to me.'

She nodded. 'I know. But I shouldn't have yelled at you like that, either. That poor lorry driver.' Her mouth twitched, and she gave a tiny ripple of laughter that was verging on tears and pressed her fingers to her lips. 'I don't know what he thought was going on.'

Joe felt a reluctant smile tug at his mouth. 'I have no idea, but I'd love to know what he told his mates.'

He saw her eyes soften, and he took a step forward and wrapped his arms gently round her and hugged her, resting his head against hers. 'I'm so, so sorry I hurt you.'

'Me, too. Can we start again? Forget any of these conversations happened and just be nice to each other?'

He lifted his head and looked down into her eyes.

'I don't know if I *can* forget that easily. You've told me too much, and whatever you say I'm going to worry about you now.'

'Don't. I'm not going to do anything rash, I'm honestly not that stupid, and I'll think really seriously about what you've said before I go any further, I promise. And I'll have another look at the donor sites.'

'No fjord cruises?' he teased, and she laughed and shook her head.

'No fjord cruises. No random one-nighters

with tall blond strangers or sneaking off into the bushes with the best man.' Her eyes were smiling now, teasing him back, and he felt himself relax. At least she wasn't still furious with him, even if the hurt he'd caused would take a while to fade.

'Good. Right, I need to go, I've got things to do before I leave.' He hesitated, then threw out his reservations and bent his head and kissed her.

Just a fleeting kiss, or it was meant to be, but then she kissed him back, her lips soft but supple, their warmth melting something deep inside him that he'd long forgotten. And so he lingered, not heating it up, but not letting her go, either. Not yet. Not for a moment...

With a mammoth effort he lifted his head, brushed his knuckles slowly over her cheek and stepped away before it was too late. 'Take care, Iona. Stay safe.'

'I will. You, too. I'll see you next week.'

He nodded, turned away, then turned back again. 'Have you got your phone on you?'

'Yes.'

'Take my number. I know what it's like when

there's nobody to bounce stuff off, and if I know nothing else, I know about sperm donation.'

She nodded, gave him a fleeting smile and keyed in his number. 'Thank you.'

'Don't thank me. Just call me if you need to.'

And with that he got back into his car, started the engine and drove away, watching her in the rear view mirror. As he got to the junction, he glanced back and she was still there, her hand raised in a little gesture of farewell.

He lifted his hand and pulled away reluctantly.

'What's happened? You look different.'

'Different?'

He bent and kissed his aunt's cheek, and she reached up and took his hand.

'Yes, different,' she said thoughtfully. 'And you didn't come yesterday.'

'I know, I'm sorry. I did let you know.'

'I know that, I got your cryptic message, but you never change your plans unless it's for work, and I knew you weren't working.'

He chuckled and sat down beside her. 'You don't miss a trick, do you?'

'No, I don't, so don't try and pull the wool over my eyes. What's going on?'

He smiled wryly and gave up. 'I've had a rather interesting weekend, what with one thing and another.'

'Have you?' she asked thoughtfully.

'Yes. I met someone on Friday. At work. A very junior registrar. She—um—she challenged my ability to do a REBOA.'

'Oh, dear—I can't imagine that went down well,' she said with a chuckle, and he gave a wry smile.

'No, not exactly. But then I borrowed her stethoscope and forgot to give it back, and when I returned it to her—well, we got talking, and to cut a long story short she's thinking about being a surrogate for her identical twin sister.'

'What—having a baby for her? Well, bless her heart. What a very brave thing to do.' She dabbed her eyes with a tissue, then tucked it back up her sleeve. 'Goodness. I can't imagine how she'll be able to do that. She must really love her sister. I could never have done anything as brave or self-less as that, even if I'd been able to.'

'No, nor me,' he said, still unconvinced she

could do it without being destroyed. 'Anyway, it was her brother's wedding yesterday, and she talked me into going with her, and her sister was there and—well, basically the sister asked her if there was any way she could convince me to be their sperm donor.'

Elizabeth's eyes widened. 'Oh! What did you say?'

He gave a wry laugh. 'All the wrong things? I accused her of inviting me to the wedding just to meet her sister—'

'Why *did* she invite you?'

'Because she found out three days before her own wedding that her fiancé was sleeping with the stripper from his stag weekend, so weddings aren't really her thing. And it was in the same church as her wedding would have been, with a lot of the same people, and she wanted me with her to deflect the sympathy. She really didn't want to go.'

She sucked in a breath and put her hand over her chest. 'Oh, the poor girl. No, I should think not. No wonder she didn't want to go alone. I'm also surprised you went.'

He laughed without humour. 'So was I.'

She plucked an imaginary bit of fluff off her sleeve, and rearranged her cardigan. 'So—are you going to do it?'

'Do what?'

'Be their sperm donor?'

'No! Elizabeth, you know how I feel about it.'

'Yes, I do, but—that's because you had no idea who the parents would be. This way, you'd know, because you've met them, so it would be different.'

'No, it wouldn't. And anyway I don't care about them. I care about Iona, and I know she thinks she's thought it through, but I'm so worried that's she's not grasped the enormity of what she's doing, that her love for Isla is blinding her to what she herself stands to lose. What if it destroys her?'

'Maybe it won't. If her sister's an identical twin, they share exactly the same genes, so it would make sense, wouldn't it, for her to be the one to carry the baby if her sister can't? Then the sister will have a child who could have been her own, and Iona will have a child she'll have a lifelong relationship with, without running the risk of another potentially messy relationship before she's ready. I can see why she's thinking like that, and it's quite unlike your situation.

'I know what you feel about your children— and, yes, before you say it, I know they're not your children, but you know what I mean. She would know the answers to all the questions you constantly ask yourself. And there's nothing to stop her further down the line meeting someone and falling in love with them and having a family of her own—someone like you, maybe?'

His aunt had the most eloquent eyes in the universe, he thought, and wouldn't hesitate to give him her opinion if she felt he'd invited it. Which he had, just by telling her. Didn't mean he liked it, especially when her eyes were saying what they were saying.

'Elizabeth, we've barely met! She's not in love with me, and I'm certainly not in love with her, and I'm not going to be.'

'No, I don't suppose you are, not after such a short time, you're much too wary. But I knew about Owen the moment I met him. It was love at first sight—'

'That doesn't exist.'

'Says the boy who couldn't work out why a

woman like Natalie would be unfaithful if she was left alone for long enough.'

'I'm not a boy, Elizabeth.'

'No, you're not. You're a man, and it's high time you stopped running away from it and having meaningless affairs and allowed yourself to be happy.'

He sighed. 'I'm not in the market for it. I'm too busy, I'm not ready for it yet, not until I've got a consultancy, if then. I'm not going to risk trashing another relationship like I did the last one.'

'Well, hopefully it wouldn't be like the last one. Hopefully she'd be rather more level headed and less egocentric, and if Iona's prepared to have a baby for her sister, I think that qualifies her quite nicely. I'd like to meet her.'

He laughed. 'Over my dead body. You know way too much about me.'

'Not if she's going to be carrying your child. She should know the kind of man you are.'

'She's not going to be carrying my child, either! And if we were in love, which we aren't, not by a country mile because we know next to nothing about each other, why would we have a baby and give it away?'

She smiled gently at him, her eyes softening. 'I wasn't suggesting that. It was a sort of either/ or. I know how hurt you are, how much Natalie destroyed your faith in women, and because of that, because I know you can't trust easily and don't want another relationship, it might be the only chance you have to bring a child into the world that you could have a relationship with.'

'No! I'm not going to do it!' And especially not now, after their row. She'd made that quite clear, and it was a miracle she'd even spoken to him again.

'Never say never. Tell me about her. What's she like?'

'Lovely. She's gorgeous,' he said honestly. 'Almost too good to be true. She's caring, very fond of all her family, but she's also spontaneous and emotional. That's why I'm worried for her, in case she's suggested this out of pity and now doesn't quite know how to retract it.'

'Maybe she doesn't want to. Maybe she'd be happy doing it. And you used to be spontaneous and emotional.'

'I know. And I learned by my mistake, and I don't want Iona to have to do the same, because as well as spontaneous and emotional, she's also either immensely brave or she's totally missed the point of what it could do to her.'

'Don't underestimate her. Women are strong, Joseph. Yes, it could hurt her, but so would not giving her sister the joy of being a mother if it's in her power. Maybe she really is that selfless. Oh, and that's the gong for tea. Lucky you, you get to run away,' she said with a twinkle in her eye that made him laugh in spite of himself.

'I need to go anyway. I've got a lot to do, I'm leaving for Manchester shortly, for this course. Would you like me to walk you along to the dining room on my way out?'

'That would be lovely, my darling. And you drive carefully, now. That car of yours has got far too much power.'

She kissed him goodbye at the dining room door, but she couldn't resist a parting shot as he walked away.

'Bring her to see me!'

He laughed. As he'd already said, over his dead body…

CHAPTER FOUR

'SO DID HE manage to track you down at the speed dating?'

Iona stared at Jenny, taking a second or two to work out what she was talking about because it seemed like a lifetime ago.

'Oh—yes. Yes, he did. Thanks for sending him there.'

'I hope he apologised for being rude in Resus as well as running off with your beloved stethoscope?'

She laughed softly. 'Yes, he apologised.' For that, and for all the things he'd said in the car, too, which had been much more hurtful. They'd come totally out of the blue and had seemed really out of character from what little she knew of him—which, she realised, was precious little, so maybe it wasn't out of character. But then he'd kissed her...

'So where am I today?'

'Oh, I think James has put you in Minors, keeping an eye on Tim. Between you and me, I think he's a bit worried about him.'

She rolled her eyes. 'He's not alone. OK, Jenny, thanks.'

She made her way to Minors, relieved in some ways that it would be a relatively easy day, but she should have realised nothing was ever as straightforward as it seemed. And Tim, with his lack of experience and apparently no gut instinct, was at the root of it.

'How are you getting on?' she asked him after a while.

'OK. I've got someone with migraine I'm just about to discharge with codeine.'

She frowned. 'Do they have a history?'

'No. It's the first time, but he said it was very bad with a roaring in his head and he was very shaky for a few minutes, so his wife brought him in.'

Iona frowned again. 'Shaky?'

'Yes—she said he was shaking all over. I assume it was from the pain.'

'Don't assume,' she said, red flags appearing

all over the place. 'Ask. Follow up. When did this start?'

'About half an hour ago, I think, or a bit more. I've done some basic neuro obs and his strength is fine.'

'Right, where is he?'

She went in, introduced herself, skipped the basic neurological strength tests and made him close his eyes and touch the tip of his nose with his index finger, first right, then left.

And he missed with the left.

'OK, it's just a precaution, but I'd like you to have a CT scan. I'll go and arrange it now.'

'A CT? Really? For a headache?' Tim asked, following her to the desk.

'Or a stroke,' she said quietly, and picked up the phone. 'Hi, I need an urgent CT on a query CVA, but he's coming up to the hour and he's got some neurological deficit. Can we send him down now?'

She put the phone down, and Tim looked shocked. 'But he's too young. He's only thirty-seven.'

'Nobody's ever too young. Let's just see what the CT comes up with.'

* * *

She was right. He had a clot in his right parietal lobe and another in the cerebellum, and was immediately whisked into the stroke unit for treatment with anticoagulants.

Tim, predictably, was shaken. 'I thought he just had a headache. His wife said it was a migraine—'

'Is she a doctor?'

'No—no, she's not. And I'm not sure I am, either.'

Iona sighed. 'Yes, you are, Tim. You just need to question everything, take nothing at face value and don't overlook the obvious. His wife said he was shaking. You should have asked what kind of shaking, because when she demonstrated it to me, it looked like a Parkinsonian tremor and that can be symptomatic of a brain injury. It's OK, I picked up on it and no harm was done, so go and get a coffee, take a break, and come back and find me. We'll work together. OK?'

He nodded, and she watched him go and let out a quiet sigh.

'Trouble in paradise?' Jenny asked, and she nodded.

'Tim misdiagnosed a stroke patient. It's OK, I picked it up in time. He's in the stroke unit.'

'Well done. So how was the wedding?'

She smiled wryly. 'OK, thanks. I went with a...friend, in the end,' she said, wondering if she would have picked up on that slight hesitation, but the red phone rang and Jenny answered it, and she escaped without any further interrogation.

Not that Jenny would really have interrogated her, but somehow she didn't want the fact that Joe had gone with her to come out, because without a doubt it would unleash a barrage of questions she didn't want to answer. She wasn't even sure she *could* answer them.

Not until she knew him better, and she suddenly realised how much she wanted that. She'd gone from thinking he was arrogant to friend to arch enemy and back to friend in the course of less than forty-eight hours, and next weekend when she'd see him again seemed a long, long way away.

The course was tough.

Tough, challenging and utterly fascinating.

Or it should have been, but for some reason he couldn't get Iona out of his mind. Iona, and her hunt for the elusive donor.

He wondered how her week was going, and if she'd looked at any more donor sites. If so, she hadn't contacted him, and he wondered if it was because she was still feeling hurt and insulted and didn't want to talk to him.

He wouldn't blame her. What an idiot. If he'd only engaged his heart instead of his mouth, he would have realised she could never have done anything that devious, but no, he'd gone straight in with all guns blazing like an arrogant idiot. Serve him right if she didn't want to speak to him again—far less ask him to be her sperm donor. Although he'd got that message, loud and clear, and so had half of East Anglia.

Damn Elizabeth for making him even consider it. There was no way—

He dragged his attention back to the lecture, forced himself to concentrate and put Iona and her surrogacy project firmly out of his mind.

The week came and went without a word from him, but then again because she'd been letting the dust settle she hadn't contacted him, either. Which meant he didn't have her phone number, she realised, because although he'd given her his, she hadn't reciprocated.

Oh, well. It was too late to ring him at ten on a Friday night, and he might be driving, or even coming back tomorrow. Or he might have been back days ago. She had no idea how long the course had been, he hadn't said, but he should be home by tomorrow. She'd call him then before her night shift and ask—just casually—how the course had gone.

Except when it came to it she didn't, because he'd said call if she needed to talk about the donor thing, and that wasn't it at all. She just wanted to hear his voice.

So she didn't call him.

And then she was in Majors on Saturday night and a patient came in with sudden acute abdominal pain, and was crippled by it. Appendix was the obvious, but she'd had it removed some years before, and she was post-menopausal so it wasn't an ectopic pregnancy, and when Iona had listened to her heart, the beat had been slightly irregular. Atrial fibrillation? Maybe, which meant she might have a clot that had been thrown out of the heart and lodged in her mesenteric artery, and that could be fatal.

She was about to arrange an urgent CT when she heard Joe's voice outside Resus, and stuck her head round the door.

'Hi. I don't suppose you've got a minute to chat about a patient, have you?'

'Sure. What's up?'

She ran through the symptoms, and he nodded. 'So what are you thinking? Acute mesenteric ischaemia from a thrombosis?'

'Maybe, and if it is I don't want to miss it.'

'No, absolutely not,' he murmured. 'CT?'

'I was about to call them when I heard your voice.'

'Let's do that now, then, if the scanner's free, and I'll take her straight to IR and sort it if you're right.'

'Call me when you have the answer.'

He grinned. 'That would be easier if I had your number,' he said, and so she rang him and heard his phone buzz in his pocket.

'OK, got it. Phone CT and tell them I'm on my way.'

'I'll get you a porter.'

'I'm sure I can manage. I'm not too posh to push,' he said with another wry grin.

'I thought that was elective Caesareans?' she retorted, and he chuckled and wheeled the patient out, taking the nurse and the notes with him.

'Good spot,' he said when he rang her twenty-five minutes later. 'She's just being wheeled into the IR suite. What time do you finish?'

'Seven thirty.'

'Me, too, technically speaking, although we both know how that goes. How do you fancy breakfast? I had a food delivery on Friday, including dry-cured bacon and massively squashy bread rolls.'

'Ooh, now... Are you offering me a bacon buttie?' she asked, her heart beating just a little faster.

'Of course.'

'Well, it's a rhetorical question then, isn't it?' she said with a laugh. 'Call me when you're done. I'll drive over.'

'I will,' he promised, and she could hear the smile in his voice and feel its echo in her lips.

'Wow. I had no idea the doors opened onto a veranda. That's fabulous!'

'It is. I love it. I sit out here whenever I can—which isn't nearly often enough, because I'm normally shut away in the study, working.'

'Can't you work out here?' she asked, peering through the doors, but he shook his head.

'Look at it. Would you do any work if you were out there?'

She laughed and turned away. 'I guess the view would be a bit of a distraction.'

'Not to mention the wildlife. The hazel tree's covered in nuts and the other day a squirrel carrying one ran from end to end of the veranda, practically over my feet. Then it dug up the lawn to bury it.'

She smiled. 'How cheeky. How are the muntjacs?'

'Noisy,' he said drily, 'but I prefer them to endless traffic noise and screaming sirens on emergency vehicles.'

She pulled out a chair and sat down at the table

to watch him while he cooked. 'I'm guessing that was London?'

'And Manchester, where I was last week. The hotel was triple glazed but I could still hear it, just a dull roar in the background. Not to mention the doors slamming all night on the corridor. I don't know why people can't shut them quietly.'

He flipped the bacon under the grill and grabbed a couple of mugs from the shelf over the cooker. 'Tea or coffee?'

'Oh—tea, please. I've had so much coffee overnight I'm wired.'

'Am I keeping you up?'

She shook her head. 'No, I need to wind down. This is perfect. So, how was the course, apart from noisy?'

'Good. Here, slit these open and butter them, the bacon's nearly done,' he added, sliding the rolls and a knife across the table. 'It was about advances in IR procedures for stroke patients. Direct access thrombolisation of the clots.'

'I had a stroke patient last week. A thirty-seven-year-old. Your course would have come in handy.'

'It would. I could have thrombolised him in

IR, which I probably wouldn't have done before this week.'

'I'll bear you in mind if I have another one. This guy nearly slipped through the net, but I rescued him from Tim, who was about to send him home on codeine.'

'Oh, dear,' he sighed, pulling a face. 'Well done, you, though. Another good spot.'

'Yes. This diagnosis thing is almost getting to be a habit,' she said lightly, and he winced.

'Was I patronising again?'

'Only slightly. I'll forgive you.'

He gave a wry laugh and stirred the tea. 'Is he OK, your patient?'

'I hope so, because we caught it within the hour so hopefully he'll be fine. No long-lasting neurological deficit, with any luck. You ought to look up his notes, see if you could have done anything.'

'Yes, I will. Good idea.' He put two mugs of tea and a plate piled with bacon down on the dining table and eyed the doors. 'Outside or in? It's chilly, but it's going to be a gorgeous day.'

'Out,' she said promptly. 'I want to meet your cheeky squirrel.'

* * *

They ate their bacon rolls on the wicker sofa outside, but the squirrel didn't show. It was still worth it, worth grabbing every moment before the Indian summer ended, and he loved it. Loved the veranda, loved the garden, loved the tranquillity after the chaos of London and his divorce.

And sharing it with Iona just made it better.

'This weather's just gorgeous,' she murmured from beside him, her feet propped on the edge of the coffee table next to his, nursing her tea in her hands. 'I can't believe it's mid-September.'

'I know, it's crazy. July and August were awful, but on the plus side I got the wall down and the doors in and the bedrooms decorated in July before the new carpets went down and I started my job.'

She turned her head and studied his face, her eyes thoughtful as if she was trying to read his mind. 'So how come you're doing all this work to your aunt's house?'

He shrugged. 'Good question. I suppose because it'll make it easier for her to let when I get a consultancy elsewhere, and ultimately it'll come to me, anyway, so I don't mind the investment. I'm her only surviving relative apart from my father, and she doesn't think he needs it. They're in a purpose-built house and he had hefty compensation for the accident, so she's probably right. And anyway, after Natalie's asset-stripping efforts, I think she feels sorry for me.'

She laughed. 'Lucky you. I'm struggling to save a deposit so I'm sharing a two-bedroomed rented flat in that converted Victorian heap. And I don't have a garden, so I'm jealous.'

He frowned. 'No access to it, or a balcony or anything?'

'No. It's the top floor, so technically I could say I live in a penthouse flat, but in reality it's an attic,' she said, her eyes crinkling in a rueful smile. 'I do have roof lights that open up to make a kind of balcony, but it's not big enough to sit there really. You ought to come and see it. I should cook for you—make a change from supermarket ready meals or the pub. Assuming we're still friends, that is?'

Her eyes were wary now, and he shook his head slowly and sighed, the memory of their argument still all too fresh in his mind. 'That's down to you, Iona, I was the one out of order, but I really hope so. Am I forgiven yet?'

A slow, teasing smile dawned on her face, lighting her eyes and bringing him an element of relief. 'Oh, I think so. You've made me bacon butties, so it would be churlish not to. And anyway,' she added, the smile fading, 'I'm blaming it on your ex.'

'Yeah, and I still do, but I'm nearly thirty-five, Iona. It's time I got over myself and stopped using her as an excuse for being suspicious about everyone's motives.'

'That's easy to say, not so easy to do. I don't want a relationship ever again, not one built on false promises and lies at any rate, and how can you possibly know until it happens? And how can you trust anyone after that? I thought Dan loved me in the way I loved him, but clearly he didn't, or he wouldn't have been shagging the stripper right before our wedding.'

'Or the umpteenth lover eighteen months after the wedding, in your own bed,' he said grimly. 'Believe me, I know exactly where you're coming from. I have no urge to get myself tied down to anyone ever again—despite my aunt's best efforts.'

She blinked at that, and laughed. 'Is she trying to set you up with one of the carers in the home?'

He chuckled and shook his head. 'No. But she wants to meet you.'

Her eyes widened. 'She knows about me?'

'Yes. I told her about you,' he admitted, 'about you wanting to have a baby for Isla. And, yes, I know I said I'd keep it to myself, but I was worried about you, and she's a doctor. She understands confidentiality, she understands childlessness, and anyway, who would she tell?'

'That's OK, I'm fine with that,' she said, to his relief. 'So what did she say?'

'She said she thought you were immensely brave. So do I, or I would if I wasn't afraid you'd get badly hurt.'

She sighed and rolled her eyes. 'Joe, I know what I'm doing, and why I'm doing it. I'm not stupid, I understand the implications, but it really won't be my baby. It'll be exactly the same as carrying Isla's embryo and a donor's. If I can ever find one, that is. I did what you said, by the way. I looked again at all the sites, read all the profiles, scoured the information given.'

'And?'

She looked back at him, then looked away again. 'There's nobody who springs out. Nobody who sounds right.'

'Isn't that for Isla and Steve to decide?'

She nodded slowly. 'Yes, I suppose it is, but they've got the same problem I have, they can't seem to find anyone that fits what they're looking for, nobody who shouts "Me!" regardless of what they look like. They've even talked about going to one of the sites where you get to meet the donors, but they're unregulated so that's not a goer, and—I know I'm dragging my heels on this, but I have so many reservations about it. Just the idea of a stranger's baby growing in my body unsettles me,' she confessed.

'If it was Steve's, it would have been a bit weird, but he's a lovely guy and I could have coped with it because it would have been giving them essentially their own baby, but that didn't work and—I don't know. Some random stranger's semen, regardless of how well screened, just makes me shudder,' she added, pulling a face, and he gave a wry laugh.

'Yeah, I can understand that it might, but if you're going to do this, there isn't really any other way apart from IVF. Have you considered trying that with Steve's sperm as the AI didn't work?'

She shook her head. 'No. I think Isla found it quite gruelling and all the embryos failed anyway, so they decided it wouldn't be fair to put me through IVF, and when the AI failed with me as well, the clinic thought it must be something to do with Steve so they suggested a sperm donor. And I hit a brick wall, and I don't know what to do or how to tell them.'

'I'm not surprised, it's a big decision.'

'I know. I just need to get over myself. Or find a donor I like the sound of, but there's only so much that information can tell you and they never seem to say enough.'

'No, I'm sure, but the profiles are hard to write. What on earth do you say about yourself that doesn't make you sound arrogant?'

'What did you say about yourself, when you did it?'

'Oh—I can't remember, I just know it was difficult.' He stood up. 'I've got a copy of it somewhere, I'll find it for you.'

He scooped up the plates and mugs, refilled the kettle and went into the study, rummaging through the filing cabinet.

'So is this where you hide out?' she asked from right behind him, making him jump.

'Are you trying to scare the pants off me?' he said with a laugh. 'Yes, it's where I hide out. I keep the blind down so I'm not distracted, and it turns it into a gloomy hole but it helps me concentrate. Here we go.'

He pulled the profile out of the file and handed it to her. 'Bear in mind I was only twenty and probably fairly full of myself.'

She took it from his hand, headed outside onto the veranda and sat down to read it, and he made more tea and went back to her.

'Well?'

'Well, you'd definitely make the short list. You give good, decent reasons for wanting to do it, you share lots of information about yourself, you aren't arrogant about your academic success or stunning good looks or physical attributes—'

'Stunning good looks? Physical attributes?' he said, preening himself a little, and she shot him a dirty look that would have worked better if she hadn't been laughing.

'Stop fishing. I didn't mean it like that. I meant some of them are, and you aren't. You almost don't say enough to sell yourself.'

'I'll take that as a compliment,' he said with a chuckle, and took it away from her. 'Drink your tea, and then I'm going to take you home. I need sleep.'

He didn't sleep.

He couldn't, because still, as it had been all week, Iona's dilemma was playing on his mind, and so was the fact that Isla had asked her about him and said he'd be perfect.

Not that she really knew anything about him, of course, so he was sure it hadn't in any way been a serious suggestion, but—what if it had been? What if she really did mean it?

He didn't want to do it again, but as Elizabeth had said, this was different, because he'd met Steve and Isla and could maybe even have a relationship with the child. And that was tugging at him in a way he hadn't expected.

Then there was the question of Iona, who'd made it quite clear what she thought of his sperm—although she'd said he'd be on the short list. Would she baulk at carrying his child?

He shut his eyes and turned over, thumping the pillow. Not *his* child. Just as none of the others out there were *his* child.

Which reminded him exactly why he wasn't going to do it again. Ever.

Not even for Iona. Assuming she'd have him.

He gave up trying to sleep, pulled on his clothes and went down to the study, and there on the desk waiting to be filed was his donor profile.

He went back upstairs, changed into shorts and trainers, plugged his ear buds into his phone and went for a ten mile run.

She didn't see him again for over a week, and then on Tuesday he sent her a text and asked if she was busy after her shift, because he wanted to discuss something. And he had food in his fridge. The last was a PS, and made her smile.

She rang him, got his answer-machine and left a message saying she'd come at seven and supper would be lovely, and then she spent the rest of her shift wondering what he wanted to talk about. Not the sperm donor thing, she knew that with absolute certainty, but what?

Was he going to suggest they have a relationship? No, he'd been clear about that. Never again. So—a no-strings affair?

No, she thought, squashing the little leap of hope. Not even he would be that premeditated. Pity…

Maybe it was work related? Something about referrals, perhaps? But then he'd do it at work. So—what, then?

She left work late, had the fastest shower on record and got to his house just after seven. He gave her a hug, then led her into the kitchen and opened the fridge.

'What do you want to drink? I've got juice, squash, cola, sparkling water, pomegranate and elderflower cordial, or I can make tea or coffee?'

'Fizzy water with a splash of cordial,' she said, dropping her bag on the table and propping herself up against the sink. 'Got any nibbles? I'm starving.'

He handed her a bag of olive breadsticks and a pot of hummus, then picked up their drinks and went out to the veranda to watch the last rays of the sunset.

'So what is it, then?' she asked, settling herself at the table and ripping the top off the hummus, and he gave a wry laugh.

'Am I that transparent?'

She crunched on a breadstick. 'Well, I haven't heard anything from you for days, and then you text me and say you want to discuss something—not did I fancy supper or you'd had an interesting case or anything like that. So it must be something else—or am I reading you wrong?' she added, studying his face.

He sighed, turned to meet her eyes and shook his head. 'Not really. I just wondered how you were getting on with the donor sites.'

'Oh, that.' She stifled her disappointment and blew on her coffee, watching the way the froth moved, creasing the pattern in the chocolate sprinkles. 'I don't know, Joe,' she sighed. 'I've still got this mental block about the stranger thing, and I'm going to have to tell Isla and Steve because I just don't think I can do it this way.'

'What if it was a friend?' he asked, his voice low, measured. Laden with meaning?

She turned her head slowly and met his eyes again, searching them in the twilight. His gaze was steady, serious. Did he…?

'I thought you said…?'

'I know, I did, but—do you think Isla was serious? About me?'

He *did* mean that. 'I'm sure she was. I didn't really think so at the time, but she's mentioned it again, and I told her about our row in the layby and the lorry driver because I thought she'd laugh, but she was gutted that she'd caused a rift between us.'

He shook his head. 'It wasn't a rift, it was me being overly defensive and running scared, feeling I'd been tricked when I thought I'd gone to the wedding to help you out of a fix that I could understand and empathise with. And I know you didn't trick me, I know you wouldn't do that, to me or to anyone. And the more I know you, the more I realise what a fool I was. I can't believe I was that stupid or that unkind.'

'So—have you seriously changed your mind about doing it again? Because you were so emphatic—'

'Not as emphatic as you. "I don't want your bloody sperm" is pretty emphatic,' he said drily. 'And maybe you meant it, but when you read my profile you said you'd put me on the shortlist, so I thought it was worth asking if you'd even contemplate carrying my baby for them, because it certainly didn't sound like it in the layby.'

Carry his baby? Her heart gave a sudden little hitch. 'I didn't mean it—not like that. I just meant I wouldn't ask you because I realised after we talked about it that you'd say no, so I never really even considered it after that, but now it seems you've changed your mind, so if you're asking me how I feel about that, then, yes, of course I would, because I know you're a really decent human being and you care about people. So the answer is, yes, I would happily carry a baby if you were the father—even if you are a bit of an idiot at times and inclined to be arrogant and patronising,' she added, smiling to soften it, 'but hey. Nobody's perfect.'

He gave a soft huff of laughter. 'Thanks—I think.'

She smiled fleetingly, then snapped a bread-stick in half and dipped it in the hummus, trying to take in what he'd said and what the implications were. 'So why the change of heart? You've been so against me doing this, spent hours trying to convince me I was making a huge mistake, and now apparently you want to be part of it? What made you think again?'

He sighed and took a breadstick from her and dunked it in the hummus. 'I don't know. Your desperation? Or, as my aunt said, because this would be different to what I did before, and it might be my only chance of having a child whose life I could have some feedback about, or maybe some involvement in? Not contact necessarily, but the odd photo, progress reports, snippets of information, that sort of thing.'

But she wasn't listening any more, she was stuck on 'only chance' because it sounded so sad, and so empty. 'Why your only chance? Did she really hurt you that badly?'

He met her eyes fleetingly and looked away, but not before she'd seen the desolation in them.

'You really need to ask that, after what you've been through and what I told you? I'm not putting myself in harm's way again, Iona. I was devastated when I caught Natalie with that guy, and to learn that he wasn't the first—no way. I'm happy to have an affair with someone who doesn't expect anything else of me, but anything that could remotely be called a relationship is definitely off limits. And I wouldn't want to have a child of my own if I wasn't in a strong, solid relationship with a woman I could trust absolutely, and I can't trust anyone, because I can't trust my own judgement—and I know you can understand that, you said it yourself the other day.

'And besides, I don't have time. I need to be able to work, to concentrate on my studies, to secure a consultancy. That's as far ahead as I'm looking at the moment, and there's no way a child features in that. So my aunt could be right. It might be my only chance to have a child and follow its progress, however remotely. And if Isla and Steve were happy with that and you felt OK with it, then—I don't know. Maybe we could meet up, get to know each other better, find out if we think it could work for us all, with any of us able to walk away if we didn't feel it could.'

She stared at him, speechless, almost over-whelmed at what he'd just said. Then she put her breadstick down, leant over and hugged him. Hard.

'Thank you. Thank you so much. I'll talk to them—ask them how they feel. They're actually coming down this weekend. How about coming to mine? They'll be staying with me because my flatmate, Libby, is away for the weekend. I could cook for us.'

'Is it big enough, or do you all want to come to me? They can see more of me, then, find out how I live, what I'm really like. You could all stay, if you wanted to. I've got plenty of room and we'd have more privacy.'

'How can you cook for four in that kitchen?'

He smiled. 'Easy. I told you, the pub does takeaways. Or we could go to the pub—neutral territory, public place, no awkward questions, just friends having a meal and a chat.' He stood up. 'Think about it. Don't say anything to them today, just think about it and talk to me again before you speak to them. You never know, you might decide you meant what you yelled at me in the layby.'

But his eyes were smiling, and he bent and brushed her cheek with his lips before he turned and walked back into the kitchen, leaving her there in turmoil, because she'd just realised that the slender hope she'd been cherishing that this might blossom into something more intimate between them had been nixed by this new development.

Sure, she was delighted for Steve and Isla, but it meant putting her own needs on the back burner, and for the first time ever, she felt a tiny twinge of resentment.

No. That was just selfish. She'd been fantasising about a bit of fun, a bit of hot sex and lazy Sunday mornings, and he'd offered her something else altogether, something much more fundamental, and possibly even more intimate.

The chance to have a child for Isla. How could she put anything above that?

CHAPTER FIVE

HE'D ASKED HER to think about it, and she did.

Constantly, for the next twenty-four hours.

She couldn't think about anything else, and the more she thought, the more convinced she was that they should do it. So she rang him as soon as she got home on Wednesday evening.

'Did you mean it?' she asked without preamble.

He didn't pretend not to understand. 'Yes, I meant it. And before you ask, yes, I'm sure. How about you?'

'Yes. I want to talk to Isla and Steve. Is that OK?'

'It's fine. Oh, and there's something you might want to tell them. I contacted the HFEA and found out about…the children.' She heard a little pause in there, almost as if he'd been about to say '*my* children' and thought better of it, but then he went on. 'Apparently there are six boys and five girls, in five families. One egg split so two of the boys are twins and they already had a daughter. The others are pairs.'

Eleven children. She felt suddenly a little breathless. 'Gosh. So they all worked. How did you feel when you found out?'

'A bit stunned? It made it all much more real. The oldest is fourteen, the youngest is eight.'

'Wow. So everything's working, then.'

'It would seem so. Anyway, feel free to pass that on. They might want to know—oh, and if they say yes, I'll go and get all the necessary checks done again to make sure everything's still all right. OK?'

'Very OK. Thank you, Joe. Thank you so much.'

'You're welcome. Right, I'm working so I need to get on. Let me know what they say.'

They were stunned.

'He said yes? But I thought—?'

'So did I, Isla, but for some reason he's changed his mind and he wants to see you again for longer, so you can get to know him and vice versa, and he suggested we all stay at his house instead of mine this weekend if you're up for that? It's out in the country, and it's lovely, and there's a great pub right on the doorstep, but if you'd rather not, if you don't feel comfortable with that, we can do it at mine—or not at all. It's up to you. There is something I haven't told you, as well, that you need to know,' she said, and told Isla all about him, his donor history, his children, then added, 'He said he'll have all the appropriate tests again before we did anything, assuming you decide you want to go ahead.'

'Wow. I had no idea. I don't know what to say. How would you feel about him being our donor?'

Her heart thumped. 'Me? I'm fine with it,' she said, trying not to think about what it might cost her in terms of a relationship with Joe, instead of what it could give her sister, which was far more important. And anyway, what relationship? He hadn't said anything about them having any other sort of relationship…

'Great. Let me talk to Steve and come back to you.'

It didn't take her long. Steve said yes immediately, and Iona rang Joe straight back as soon as they were off the phone.

'They said yes, they'd love to meet up. Are you sure about it being at yours?'

'Yes, that's fine, but I'm working on Friday night so if you all come over at say two on Saturday, after lunch? That should give me a few hours to sleep, but I'm off all day Friday so I can sort out the house and do a food order. If I book it now we can go to the pub on Saturday evening and I'll do breakfast.'

'Let me pay for the food.'

'No. This was my idea. Right, back to the paperwork— Ah. Any dietary things I need to know?'

'No. Totally omnivorous, like me. They're not fussy.'

'Great. Right, well, I'll see you on Saturday,' he said.

After he'd hung up she sat motionless, staring blindly out of the window, her thoughts in freefall.

It was going to happen. If they all got on, and she couldn't see why they wouldn't, she might end up having a baby. Unless she didn't get pregnant with Joe, either. Maybe there was something wrong with her, too?

Well, it looked like she was going to find out—assuming the weekend was a success.

There was a strange, tight feeling in her chest. Fear?

No. Not fear. There was nothing to fear. It would be fine.

Maybe—anticipation?

Ten to two.

Would they be early? Late? Right on time? Iona had been late once, but that was because of work. Would they bring two cars? He'd put his in the garage out of the way, so there was room for two just in case.

The fridge was full, the house was clean, the beds were made, the dishwasher, his only concession to a new kitchen, was on. He glanced at the clock again.

Seven minutes to two.

His palms prickled, and he realised he was nervous. Nervous that they wouldn't like him, or nervous that they would? He felt as if he was about to be interviewed, but he'd been through that process before and passed the clinic's test.

Not with the intended parents, though. Although they would have seen his—

Profile. Damn. He'd updated it last night at work in an oddly quiet interlude, but he hadn't printed it.

Too late. He heard the crunch of tyres on gravel, doors slamming, voices, and he un-clenched his fists, walked into the hall and opened the front door.

Iona was there, Isla and Steve beside her, and they all looked as nervous as he felt.

He stifled the laugh, stepped back and wel-comed them in. He had a weird moment when he didn't know how to greet them, but Isla took the decision out of his hands and gave him a quick, warm hug and kissed his cheek.

'This is so kind of you, Joe,' she said softly, her eyes so like Iona's that he felt he could read every emotion in them—and there were plenty.

'I just felt it would be easier for all of us. We've got more space here, room to get away from each other if necessary.'

Isla returned his smile, her face relaxing slightly. 'I'm sure it won't be.'

'I hope not. Steve—good to see you again.' He

shook his hand, felt the firm, warm grip, met the clear blue eyes that searched his and maybe found what they were looking for, because he smiled, his face relaxing just as Isla's had.

'You, too. And thank you so much for inviting us here.'

'You're welcome. Hi, Iona. You OK?'

She nodded, hesitated a moment and then gave him a quick hug. 'You?'

'I'm fine. Come on through.'

He made coffee, and they took it in the sitting room and he answered all their questions, and they answered his. So many questions, Iona thought, and the more openly they talked, the more she realised what a good fit he was with them.

They felt so much the same about so many things, and whether you believed in nature or nurture, that was important. Biologically his role, like hers, was clearly defined, to provide Isla and Steve with a child as genetically close to their own as possible. OK, he wasn't a dead ringer for Steve, but apart from his hair colour he wasn't a million miles off and other things were more important. And, as Joe had so succinctly put it, they were both just a means to an end—and that end was now in sight. So she took herself off into the kitchen, put the kettle on again and made a pot of tea.

She'd baked a cake this morning while she'd waited for them to arrive, and she went out to the car and brought it in, just as Joe came out of the sitting room.

'Wow, that looks good.'

'I hope so. It's my mother's apple cake recipe and it's usually pretty reliable. So how's it going?'

He shrugged. 'OK, I think. They haven't got back in the car yet, at least.'

That was said with a slight lift to his lips, not quite a smile, but his eyes were gentle and she put the cake down, put her arms around him and hugged him.

'I'm so grateful to you for doing this,' she mumbled into his chest.

'They haven't said yes yet.'

'They will. Cake?'

'Definitely. I haven't eaten since last night.'

'No lunch?'

He shook his head. 'I wasn't hungry. The nights mess with my body clock.'

She felt her mouth tilt. 'I reckon you're saving yourself for Maureen's fish and chips. Did you book a table for tonight or did you forget?'

He laughed and got some plates out. 'No, I didn't forget. Our table's booked for seven thirty. Is that OK?'

'Sounds fine. We've brought walking shoes, by the way. I thought maybe we could go for a stroll after we've had cake?'

He nodded. 'Great idea. It's easier to talk while you're walking. No eye contact. You can say the things that are harder to say face to face.'

'What, like "no"?'

He laughed again. 'Hopefully not, although it's down to them. Shall we have tea on the veranda?'

'So, did I pass?'

They were standing in the hall, bags packed and ready to go, after what he hoped had been a good and constructive weekend. He'd meant to leave it up to them to tell him how they felt after they'd had time to consider it, but the suspense had got the better of him.

Isla's jaw dropped, and then her eyes filled. 'Did *you* pass? I thought you were vetting us? Did *we* pass?'

He laughed, the tension going out of him like air out of a punctured balloon. 'Of course you passed. That was never in question. And—if you decide to go ahead, I just hope it works for you, because I've seen the grief of childlessness at first hand, and I wouldn't wish it on anyone,' he added quietly.

'Thank you. Thank you so much.' Steve hesitated a second, then wrapped his arms around Joe and hugged him hard. 'You're a good man.'

Steve let him go, and he caught Iona's eye and she winked at him and turned to the others. 'Well, if you've all finished your mutual love-in, maybe we'd better get on the road because you've got a long journey back and I'm absolutely sure Joe has a heap of work he wants to do before tomorrow.'

They said their goodbyes, Iona kissed his cheek and whispered, 'Thank you,' and he closed the door, turned around and leant on it with a sigh of relief.

He was drained. Physically, mentally and emotionally exhausted, and oddly flat, because—ah, no point thinking about what might have been with Iona. This was far more important than scratching an itch, and she was turning into a cherished friend. He should concentrate on that, be there for her, not worry about what he might or might not be missing. And anyway, he wasn't ready for that and she deserved better than what he could offer. He'd already proved that with his stupid accusations after the wedding.

He levered himself away from the door and went into the kitchen. It was a mess, strewn with the remains of brunch. He emptied and reloaded the dishwasher, switched it on and went out onto the veranda, too tired to think about working.

The Indian summer seemed to be lingering indefinitely, and it was a beautiful early October day. He lay down on the wicker sofa, shifted the cushions until he was comfortable and closed his eyes. Just five minutes...

* * *

He was fast asleep.

He hadn't answered the doorbell, so she'd walked round the side and there he was, sprawled out across the sofa, one foot on the ground, his other leg draped over the end, sleeping like a baby.

She perched on the chair by his feet and waited, but it wasn't until the squirrel ran along the veranda and its tail whisked past his trailing hand that he woke with a start.

'Iona? I didn't know you were here. What was that?'

She was laughing. 'The squirrel. Its tail brushed you.'

He yawned hugely and sat up, stretching, and she sat down beside him on a nice warm patch. 'Are you OK?'

He nodded, his eyes still looking a little bleary. 'Yeah. I'm just exhausted. It was a long night at work on Friday, and it was quite tough being on my best behaviour all weekend. How are they?'

'They love you. They think you're amazing. So do I.'

'So—are we going to do this? Subject to my test results coming back OK?'

'It looks like it. When are you having them done?'

'I did it on Friday. I thought I'd get ahead of the game, just make sure, you know? Since Natalie—well, I've been a bit phobic, so I had a sexual health screen straight away and another one six months later just to be sure nothing had been missed, but they were all clear, so I guess I got away lightly. And before you ask, no, I haven't had sex with anyone, unprotected or otherwise, since then. It was the semen analysis I wanted to check to make sure all the little swimmers are up to speed, just so I don't waste anybody's time.'

'So when will you know that?'

'Couple of days? It shouldn't be long. What about you? Have you had any screening ever?'

She laughed a little unsteadily. 'Oh, I got checked out eighteen months ago after I dumped Dan, and again before I started this process, just to be on the safe side. And, no, neither have I, before you ask,' she added with a smile.

He smiled back understandingly. 'Good. So,

if we get a definite yes from Isla and Steve, I guess we wait for you to ovulate—if you're absolutely sure you want to do this?'

'I'm sure. For what it's worth, you might want to put Saturday week into your calendar,' she said, feeling suddenly a little embarrassed and not quite meeting his eyes—which in the great scheme of things was ridiculous, as they'd just been talking about his little swimmers. She stood up and headed for the kitchen.

'I don't suppose there's any cake left? It's a long time since we had brunch.'

She heard the wicker sofa creak, and he followed her into the kitchen, coming up behind her and putting his hands on her shoulders. She turned into his arms and rested her head on his chest, listening to the steady beat of his heart under her ear, feeling the warmth seep through her. She wanted more, so much more, but he hadn't ever suggested it, and now with this new relationship, it would be crazy to contemplate—

'Stay for dinner,' he said softly. 'I've hardly seen you recently.'

'You've been working.'

'I'm always working. Stay anyway.'

She lifted her head and looked up at him, noticing the slight stubble coming through, wondering how it would feel against her skin…

'You just want me to cook for you,' she said accusingly, trying not to smile, and she felt his chest vibrate slightly as he chuckled.

'Rumbled. Why don't we go to the pub? They do a great Sunday roast. And they clear up their own kitchen.'

'Sold. And I'm buying.'

They said yes. An unequivocal, definite, gold-plated yes.

His results were good—his sperm quality was excellent, apparently—and then came the wait, and she found it almost unbearable.

Would it happen this time? Would she, in the next few weeks, find out that she was pregnant?

She was due to ovulate on Saturday, a fortnight after Isla and Steve had left, but where and how they were going to do this hadn't been decided. It wasn't going to be made any easier to schedule it as she was supposed to be working on that Saturday, and yet again in the week before they were both busy and working conflicting shifts, so there didn't seem to be a good time to meet and discuss it. And then, on the Thursday night before *that weekend*, she rang him.

'Are you still OK for this weekend?' she asked, and she heard a grunt of what could have been laughter.

'Yes, I'm fine. I was thinking we should do it here. It's easier than at your flat with Libby there. Much more privacy, and we'll probably both be more relaxed. So—what time do you finish work on Saturday?'

'I don't know. Hopefully before seven.'

'So how about straight afterwards? You could come here and I'll cook us a meal and then afterwards when it's done you can stay over. Unless you've got a better idea?'

'No, that sounds fine. Are you sure about this? All of it?' she asked again, and he said yes without hesitation.

'Sure?'

'Yes, Iona. I'm sure. You're right, they're great people, and I'm less worried about you than I was because you're really close to them, so you'll have lots of contact with the child and you'll be able to see the huge difference it'll make to their lives. They were adamant about that, about wanting you to be a big part of the child's life, and that takes away a lot of my concerns. So, yes, I am sure, not only for you or me, but for the child, too. They'll be the perfect family. I couldn't ask for more than that. So stop worrying, and I'll see you on Saturday evening.'

She was nervous.

Nervous, awkward and a little embarrassed, for him as much as for herself. She packed a few things—including, for no good reason, a pretty raspberry pink silk nightie with shoe-string straps and little lace inserts. She'd never worn it, but for some reason it seemed appropriate, and it would be the only touch of romance in a soulless clinical procedure, so she threw it into the bag, zipped it up and headed over to his.

He opened the door before she was out of the car, and she met his eyes through the windscreen and felt a flicker of panic. Not doubt, it wasn't that, she'd never doubted for a minute that this was the right thing to do, but getting through the next hour or two might be a bit of a challenge.

She got out of the car, locked it and headed towards him, trying to smile. 'Hi.'

'Hi,' he said, his voice soft and low and slightly gravelly. 'You OK?'

'Yes, I'm fine,' she lied. 'Something smells good.'

'I made lamb shanks. They've been in the slow cooker for hours, they'll be ready soon. Do you want to put your bag upstairs and settle in? I've put you in the room you had before.'

Her heart thumped a little, and she nodded. 'Thanks. I'll do that now.'

She ran upstairs, opened the door and paused. He'd closed the curtains and turned on the bedside lights, bathing the room in a soft, golden glow. He'd even changed the bedding, although she'd only slept in it for one night. She put her bag down, then sat on the edge of the bed and ran her hand absently over the soft cotton. So this was where it would happen, the thing that hopefully would change Isla and Steve's lives and give them what they wanted more than anything in the world.

Fingers crossed.

She could hear music playing downstairs,

soft and relaxing, and she went down again and found him in the kitchen. He turned and smiled at her.

'Glass of wine?'

'Oh—that would be lovely,' she said, and he handed her a glass.

'Try that. It's a nice smooth Rioja. Or if you don't like it, I've got others, but I thought it would go well with the lamb.'

She sipped, nodded and smiled. 'That's really nice.'

'Good. Come on, let's go and sit down and chill for a minute before we eat. There's no rush.'

There were crisps in a bowl on the coffee table, and she scooped up a few, kicked off her shoes and settled into a corner of the sofa with her legs curled under her. 'So are you going to give me the third degree again?' she asked after a silence that stretched out too long for her comfort, and he laughed.

'No, Iona, I'm not going to give you the third degree. I've told you I'm fine with it. This is your decision, you've obviously all thought it through carefully and sensibly, and I'm just here to provide the means.'

'That's a big "just",' she pointed out, and his eyes softened in another smile.

'Let's face it, you're the one who's got the tough job. I'm just going to have a couple of minutes of fun.'

She felt a faint brush of colour sweep over her face, and she dropped her eyes and twiddled her wine glass between her fingers for a moment. 'It's more than that—much more. I know you had huge reservations about doing this again—'

'I'm over them. This is different, and I'm sure Isla and Steve will be amazing parents. I have no reservations about that at all. My only concern is you—'

'Joe, I'm fine—'

'Right now you are, but I want you to know that you can always talk to me about it, whenever you need to, day or night, and if you need any help while you're pregnant, if it happens, then I'll be here for you. You won't be alone.'

She felt her eyes fill, and swallowed. 'Thank you,' she said, her voice little more than a whisper. Not because she felt she'd need help, but because he'd offered it unsolicited when he really hadn't needed to.

A beeping noise sounded from the kitchen, and he went through, telling her to stay where she was, but she was restless, so she uncurled herself and got to her feet, studying the books on the bookshelf, the CDs and DVDs in the rack, the photographs she'd never looked at before.

His parents, she realised, seeing a man in a wheelchair with a woman leaning over the back of it and laughing down at him. They looked the picture of happiness, but she knew that that happiness was the bedrock of a marriage that had been tried to its limit.

There was another photo, the woman looking strikingly similar to his father, and to Joe. His aunt? The man beside her was tall and gaunt and unsmiling, but his arm was curled protectively around her and she was leaning into him with a contented smile on her face.

What a contrast his own marriage had been. It must have been such a shock to discover that not everyone was so happy, so committed, so much in love. She knew exactly how that felt...

'Ready when you are,' he said, sticking his head round the door, and then he saw what she was looking at and came over to her. 'My parents, Bill and Mary, and my aunt and uncle, Elizabeth and Owen.'

'I'd worked that out.'

'Had you, Sherlock?'

'I had. It took some deduction, but it was the strong family resemblance that gave me the clue.' She smiled up at him, and he laughed softly and steered her out of the sitting room into the kitchen.

The food was delicious, the lamb meltingly tender, the rainbow of vegetables clean and fresh, a perfect foil for the rich sauce. He'd served it on a bed of crushed baby potatoes drizzled in olive oil, and she ate every bite.

'That was amazing. You're a really good cook—or else you got it from the pub and reheated it,' she teased, and he laughed despairingly and rolled his eyes.

'Oh, ye of little faith. I cooked it from scratch, I'll have you know. I am housetrained. It's Elizabeth's recipe. She's the one who taught me to cook.'

'Your aunt, not your mother?'

He nodded. 'My mother was too busy looking

after my father then, so I spent a lot of time here with my aunt and uncle while I was growing up, and it was a happy time. There's a playground on the other side of the stream that runs down the side, and my uncle made a little makeshift bridge over it so I could go there. I spent hours there, either on my own or playing with the other children in the village.'

'Is that why you took the job in Yoxburgh? So you could come back to the place where you'd been so happy?'

He nodded again, thoughtfully this time. 'Yes—I suppose it was. I wanted to be near for her anyway, but I have very fond memories of my time here, and it was a no-brainer when the job came up at the right time. And I might even get a consultancy if they expand the department.'

'When will you finish all your exams?'

'By next summer, and then I'll be looking for a post, but fingers crossed I get one near enough so I can still see her regularly. If it wasn't for her it wouldn't matter where I went, but I think it comforts her to know I'm near so I don't want to go far. My parents are younger and they've got each other, but since Owen died she's been alone and I think she finds losing her independence difficult, too. And she likes the intellectual stimulation of discussing medical issues with me—says it keeps her brain on its toes. Whatever, she's always pleased to see me.'

'I'm sure she is. I'd love to meet her. She sounds a wonderful woman.'

'She is. She was a GP before women doctors were the norm, and she had to fight hard to get where she did. But I'm not sure I'm going to introduce you. She knows way too much about me and I have no doubt she'd be more than happy to share. Pudding?'

'You've got pudding? I'm stuffed!' she said regretfully.

'That's a shame. I've made chocolate mousse, and I've picked the last fresh raspberries from the garden.'

'Ooh. Well, in that case it would be rude not to...'

And then finally there was nothing else to talk about, nothing more to do but face the reason they were there together.

He put his glass down on the table, met her

eyes and smiled gently, as if he understood how she was feeling. 'Why don't you go upstairs and have a nice hot shower and get ready?' he said softly, and she nodded and went up, unpacked her bag and took out the little pot and the syringe she'd bought in readiness. Then she found her wash things and went into the bathroom.

There was a clean towel on the side of the bath, and she locked the door—crazy, really, because there was no way he'd come in—then stripped off, twisted her hair up out of the way and stepped under the steaming water.

For a long moment she just stood there letting it wash over her, and then slowly, as if she was preparing herself for some fertility ritual, she reached for the shower gel and lathered herself carefully, paying attention to every square inch of her body, readying herself for the momentous thing she was about to do.

It seemed curiously important that she should do this right, should prepare herself, body and mind, as if it would make her body more receptive.

She knew she was ovulating. She'd felt a tugging pain low down on the left earlier that day, so her body was ready.

All she needed now was Joe…

She stepped out of the shower onto the thick, fluffy bathmat and wrapped herself in the towel. Egyptian cotton? Probably. He liked the good things in life.

Then she gathered up her things, went back to the bedroom and dried herself, then slipped on the hopelessly romantic silk nightie that she'd never worn before, stifling a pang of regret that he wouldn't see her in it, that they wouldn't do this thing the way her heart and her body were crying out to do it. There was a fluffy towelling robe on the back of the door and she put it on and belted it firmly over the nightie, took a steadying breath and opened the door.

CHAPTER SIX

HE'D SHOWERED DOWNSTAIRS, towel-dried his hair and pulled on clean lounge pants and a T-shirt, and now he was waiting.

How was she feeling?

Weird, probably. He certainly felt weird. This was so different to doing it anonymously in a clinic, but he'd just have to shut his mind to all the tumbling thoughts and do the job.

He glanced down at his body. 'You'd better co-operate,' he told it, and then he heard her door open and her voice calling him.

He took a deep breath, let it out slowly and walked out of his room.

She was perched on the edge of the bed wrapped in the robe, but he could see a sliver of thigh at the hem and in the gaping neck he could make out a flimsy bit of dark pink silk and lace above a shadowed cleavage, and his body leapt to life. Well, that would make things easier, he thought wryly, but she wasn't looking at him, just sitting there on the edge of the bed staring at the floor, and beside her on the bedside table was a little pot and a syringe.

He swallowed. 'Are you OK?'

She nodded, but she didn't look up and he wondered if she was embarrassed. Or if she'd changed her mind about him?

He dropped down onto his haunches in front of her and put his hands on her knees over the robe. 'What's wrong? Is it still making you shudder?'

'No. No, it's nothing. It just—it all seems a little soulless, that's all. I know it's stupid because it couldn't possibly know, but—it just seems such a clinical and loveless way to make a baby...'

She glanced at the pot, then away again, and he put a finger under her chin and lifted her head gently until he could see her eyes.

They were soft and luminous in the light from the lamp, shimmering with unshed tears.

'It isn't loveless,' he said softly. 'You're doing this out of love for your sister and your brother-in-law. Just think of that, of them.'

She swallowed and nodded. 'Yes. Yes, you're right, I'm only being silly, but it just seems so cold—'

She broke off, took a deep breath and looked him in the eye. 'Go on, then. Go and do your stuff. I'll be all right.'

He picked up the pot and straightened up, then glanced back at her. She was hugging herself, her arms wrapped tightly round her waist as if she was holding herself together, and he replaced the pot, sat down beside her and put his arm round her.

She was as taut as a bowstring, and he shook his head and dropped a kiss on her hair.

'Hey, Iona, it's OK. We don't have to do this if you're not sure.'

'I am,' she said, her voice small and clogged with tears. 'I'm just being ridiculous.'

'It's not ridiculous, it's a huge step. Or is it me? Am I the problem?'

She looked up at him again, her eyes like windows. 'No—no, it's not you. Definitely not you.' She sighed wistfully and looked away. 'I always used to dream of falling in love and getting married and having babies, and I don't ever seem to have got past the first one, and maybe there's a bit of me that wants to do this for them because like you it might be my only chance to have a baby. And at least I won't have to change nappies.'

She was laughing at that, but it was such a sad little laugh it tore him in two, because he'd had the same dream of happy-ever-after once, and Natalie had snatched it from him and turned it into a nightmare.

'I can understand that,' he said. 'I had that dream, and it was destroyed. It's like she took my innocence and burnt it alive in front of my eyes and left me unable to trust or love anyone.'

She looked up at that, reached up, cradled his jaw with her hand, a little frown creasing her brow. 'I'm so sorry she hurt you.' Her fingers were icy, and he realised she was shivering, although it wasn't cold. He turned his head a fraction, pressed his lips into her palm.

'Let's go downstairs and talk about it, hmm?'

'No. No, Joe, I want to do this now,' she said, her voice much firmer. 'I'm just being a drama queen, but you're right, I'm doing it for love, and it's not as if the baby's going to notice how it gets there, is it?'

He looked at the pot, looked at her determined but wistful face, and threw his sanity out of the window.

'There is an easier way,' he said softly, and she turned and looked up at him, her eyes confused as they searched his.

'Easier—?' And then her eyes widened, her lips parted, her soft gasp barely audible. 'You'd do that?'

'Why not? I'm not in a relationship, neither are you, and neither of us has any reason to want one at this time in our lives, but that doesn't mean we aren't still normal, healthy adults, and there's no way I'm going to deny that I want you, Iona. I have done, right from day one. You're beautiful, in every way, so, yes, I'd do that, without hesitation. So long as you don't expect anything else from me, and so long as you don't do anything crazy like imagine you're in love with me, then I'm more than happy to have a no-strings affair with you.

'But you do need to understand the rules. This isn't happy-ever-after, Iona. This is just what it is, an honest, straightforward physical relationship between two like-minded people, and if it leads to a baby for your sister, that's good. If it doesn't, I'm still happy, but it's not for ever and you need to know that up front. I'm not and I never will be again in the market for happy-ever-after, so it's entirely your call.'

She searched his eyes, felt a shiver of need run through her and her breath caught in her throat.

'OK. And—yes.'

'Are you absolutely sure?'

She nodded. 'I'm sure.'

He stood up, pulled her to her feet and cupped her shoulders in his hands, staring down into her eyes. He must have seen what he was looking for, because he lowered his head—slowly, as if he was giving her time to back away—and then she went up on tiptoe and closed the gap.

Her mouth met his and it felt—hot. So hot, soft yet firm, and hungry. So hungry. Flames shot through her and she parted her lips for him, her tongue meeting his and searching, exploring the taste and feel of him as he kissed her back.

Mint, cool and clean, contrasting with the heat

of his tongue, the warmth of his hands on her back. He slid one down, cradled her bottom and she tasted his groan as he lifted her against him.

She felt the hard ridge of his erection, the tautness of his spine beneath her hands, the softness of his hair as she threaded her fingers into it and pulled his head down towards her. He hadn't shaved, and she felt the slight rasp of his beard against her skin, the sensation sending fire dancing through her veins.

He eased away, sliding the gown off her shoulders. She heard the sharp hiss of his indrawn breath, then his hands traced her body through the silk and lace, the heat of his palms setting fire to her everywhere they touched.

'I want you,' he breathed, his lips leaving hers, teasing her throat, his breath drifting hot and urgent over her skin.

His hands cupped her bottom and he rocked against her, making her gasp and clench her legs together against the sudden blizzard of sensations. She'd never felt—

'You're shivering,' he said, and letting go of her he flicked back the covers. 'Get into bed, you're freezing,' he said, his voice gruff, and she lay down, staring up at him, seeing the need raw in his eyes as he stripped off his clothes and rested one knee on the edge of the bed, his body taut and proud, aroused.

Her heart pounded, her breathing short and tight, and then he reached out a hand and ran it lightly over her breast, and she thought her heart would stop.

The nipple peaked instantly under the silk and his eyes darkened, the ice turning to fire. 'You're beautiful, do you know that? So beautiful,' he said rawly, and then he was there beside her, wrapping the covers over them and reaching for her again.

His mouth found hers, then moved on, trailing fire over her throat, her collar bones, down between her breasts. He turned his head a fraction, caught her nipple between his lips, flicked it with his tongue through the fine silk and then blew on it, cooling it again.

A shudder ran through her and her hands plucked at him, running over his hot, smooth skin, down his back, up again and round, her fingers trailing over his hip, down, across a board-flat abdomen, finding their target.

He gave a shuddering groan as her fingers closed around the hot, straining shaft of his erection, and his hand found the edge of lace and slid under it, his hot palm flat against the bowl of her pelvis. She rocked, arching up towards him, and his hand moved down, one knee nudging her legs apart to give his skilful fingers access.

She should have known. She'd seen how sensitive his fingers were, almost instinctive, and his touch was unerring as he gently explored the delicate folds. How did he know how to touch her, to turn her body into liquid fire?

'Joe—!'

'Shh. I'm here. I've got you,' he breathed, and then his mouth found hers again and he moved over her, their bodies merging into one. She could feel his heart beat against her chest, breathed his air as he held his face just over hers, their eyes locked as he started to move, picking up the rhythm of the silent drumbeat of their bodies.

She felt the beat quicken, felt his instant response, the driving, thrusting urgency of his movement as his body surged against hers over and over again as she rose to meet him, and then he found her mouth again, his teeth nipping gently, his tongue thrusting, faster and faster as her body exploded into a million shards of light.

She felt him stiffen, felt the deep, pulsing shudder of his climax, felt the groan torn from deep inside his chest, his head dropping against her shoulder. His body went limp for a moment as he caught his breath, and then he propped himself up on his elbows and stared down into her eyes.

He looked as shocked as she felt, stunned by the force of what they'd unleashed, but then he lowered his head and touched a gentle kiss to her mouth before rolling to his side and gathering her tenderly into his arms, while the aftershocks rolled through them and their hearts slowed.

'Wow,' he murmured softly, brushing a hand lightly over her hair and sifting the fine, silky strands through his fingers. 'Where did that come from?'

'I don't know, but I'm not complaining.'

Her voice sounded stunned, and he chuckled. 'Me neither,' he murmured, hugging her closer and trying to work out what had happened.

And then she laughed a little unsteadily. 'I

know one thing, if I am pregnant it's a good job the baby won't know how it got there,' she said, and his gut clenched.

The baby. He'd forgotten about the baby.

He'd started out with the best intentions, but then somewhere along the line he'd forgotten why they were doing it, what it was all about, and concentrated on wringing every last ounce of exquisite pleasure out of it for both of them.

Well, he'd certainly done that, and whatever else it might have been, it certainly hadn't been soulless.

'I think maybe some things are best left unsaid,' he told her, his voice sounding rusty, and then sucked in his breath as another shockwave rippled through his body. He felt blindsided, totally confused. He'd never felt like this in his life, so right, so connected, so—perfectly in tune. And it had come out of nowhere, just when he'd committed himself to looking after her.

And it was too late to change his mind, too late to realise that making love to her was a big mistake. Because it had felt like making love, not having sex, and if it hadn't been for his commitment to her he would have run a mile.

But he couldn't do that, because he'd made her a promise, and he didn't break his promises. There was no way he could walk away from her, not now, and he realised he didn't really want to. He wanted to stay with her, see her through her pregnancy, if there was one, enjoy the next few months, and then move on as planned.

They could still have the relationship he'd outlined to her, based on a mutual understanding, and then when the time was right they'd both move on, her to handing over the baby if there was one and getting her life back on track, him to furthering his career.

But he knew, in his heart of hearts, that she would be a hard act to follow, and suddenly nine months didn't seem anything like long enough.

Better make the most of it...

She stirred, waking slowly from a heavy sleep, and then blinked, confused for a moment until it all came back to her.

The room was in semi-darkness, the only light coming from the landing through the slightly open door. Joe must have turned off the lights,

she realised, and reached for him, only to find
he'd gone.

Gone some time ago, as well, if the cool sheets
were anything to go by, and she felt oddly bereft.
Stupid, really. It was only sex, he'd made that
clear enough, and the only reason she was there
at all was because he'd offered to help her sister.

She had no hold over him, no rights to any ex-
pectations, and she knew that. She'd agreed to
it, but it hadn't taken her long to work out how
little her promise to him had registered with her
heart.

Where was he? Not her business, but she
needed the bathroom. Maybe that was where
he was?

She lay there for a while, but the house was silent, and she turned on the light and rummaged
for her phone.

Four thirty-eight. Had he woken and gone back
to his own room? She slipped out of bed, pulled
on the robe and crept out of the door, trying not
to disturb him, but his bedroom door was open,
the bed untouched. And the light was on in the
hall below.

She used the bathroom and then went downstairs, followed the light and found him in his study, sitting on the sofa with the laptop on his lap and a mug in his hand. He'd pulled his clothes back on, but his feet were bare and curiously sexy, and she felt a little awkward. Was she supposed to feel that? Or was she out of line, following him down here to see what he was doing? Maybe he hadn't wanted her to. Was that what he'd meant by not getting any ideas? She didn't have a clue.

She hovered there in the doorway for a moment, not knowing what to say and wondering if she should quietly slip back upstairs and pretend she hadn't been down, but he looked up and met her eyes a little warily.

'Hi. You OK?'

She nodded. 'I wondered where you were. I might have known you'd be working. Is the kettle still hot?'

'I doubt it. Do you want tea?'

'I can make it,' she said, and he held the mug out to her. 'Is that "Please can I have another one"?' she asked lightly, going over to take it, and he grinned and put the mug down and caught her hand.

'It could be,' he said, closing his laptop. 'Or we could get a glass of water and go back up to bed, which is my preferred option.'

She felt the tension go out of her like a punctured balloon, and he pulled her onto his lap so that she straddled him, threaded his fingers through her hair and drew her head down so he could kiss her. She felt his body change instantly, felt hers responding, then without warning he stood up, cradling her bottom in his hands, and carried her upstairs to bed.

'Right, where were we?' he asked gruffly, sitting down on the bed. She was still straddling him, the contact intimate and yet not— until his hands slid up under the gown, under the nightie, shifting her as he tugged down his trousers. Then he settled her back down and rocked against her, just gently, just enough to drive her wild.

He shifted again, his fingers—those clever, wicked fingers—stroking, searching until she thought she was going to die if he made her wait another second—

And then he was there, filling her, making her gasp and fall forward, her hair tumbling across his chest as he lay back and tunnelled his fingers through it, tilted her face and kissed her.

So much for her doubts, she thought, and then felt herself tighten, felt sensation crashing through her as he rolled her onto her back and drove into her one last time, and then she lost all coherent thought...

They woke up starving, and he showered quickly and went down to start breakfast while she followed him through the bathroom.

It seemed a lifetime ago that she'd showered in there, in preparation for what had turned out to be the most amazing night of her life. She smiled and hummed to herself as she washed, a little part of her wondering if deep within her body a tiny life was starting.

No. It would be too soon—wouldn't it? Better not to think about it yet. She'd done that before and it hadn't worked.

She turned off the water, towelled herself quickly dry, pulled on her jeans and a light sweater and ran downstairs in bare feet.

'Perfect timing. Veranda?'

'Lovely. I'll get socks,' she said, and ran back

up to get them. She put her trainers on, too, and threw her things back into her bag and took it down with her, dumping it by the front door.

'Right, breakfast,' she said, going out onto the veranda, and he touched his finger to his lips and pointed down the garden.

A small deer was there, nuzzling the ground under the sweet chestnut tree at the bottom of the garden, and as she took a step forward it lifted its head, turned and vanished into the shrubs.

'Does chestnut stuffing go with venison?' she asked, tucking into a bacon roll, and he chuckled.

'I don't know, but it woke me last night so I might yet find out. That was when I got up, a little after three. I was awake, and—well, there's always work to do.'

'There is—for you, anyway. I'm all packed. I'll eat this and head off, leave you to get on.'

'I won't do much, I need to go to bed at some point. I'm on nights all week, starting tonight, so I'll work in the quiet spells. It's not usually that busy, it's just for covering the out of hours stuff, so it might be fairly useful because I've got an exam at the end of next week.'

'I don't suppose I'll see much of you in the next few days, then,' she said, trying to keep it light and not sound needy, but he shrugged.

'I don't know. I would say if you were going to get pregnant this weekend we've probably done enough, unless you want to wake me up at five,' he murmured with a lazy, wicked twinkle.

Her heart thumped at that reminder of why they were doing this, and although she wanted to say yes, she knew that she had to keep some distance for the sake of her sanity. So she said no. 'I'm tempted, but I think you probably need to concentrate on work and sleep for the rest of the week,' she told him with a smile to soften it.

'Maybe next weekend, then? We'll have to see how it goes. If I haven't got enough work done for the exam, I'll need to study all weekend as well. Want another?' he offered, and she took another bacon roll.

'You make the best bacon butties in the world,' she mumbled round a mouthful, and he chuck-led.

'I do, don't I?' he agreed, and sank his teeth into another one.

* * *

She didn't see him again that day, although she was tempted to go back and wake him as he'd suggested, but she thought better of it and it was just as well because it turned out he'd gone and visited his aunt and wouldn't have been there anyway.

And the nights that followed apparently weren't as quiet as he'd hoped, so he ended up having to work all the following weekend.

Did she mind? Yes. Did it matter? No. She had no rights, no claim on his time or attention, and she had no urge to distract him from his work, but she began to get a glimmer of how Natalie might have felt left alone so much.

Not that she was much better. She had study of her own to do over the weekend after a one-day course down in London that Thursday, and apart from sporadic texts and emails they didn't talk.

She caught up with him finally in the ED on Tuesday afternoon of the week of his exam, when she was struggling to get a line into a very sick little girl. She'd been brought in by her anxious parents and not a minute too soon. She was floppy and pale, seriously dehydrated after forty eight hours of gastroenteritis, and Iona couldn't get a line in anywhere.

She'd tried to find a vein, so had Jenny, there wasn't a paediatrician free to come and do it and she was about to call Sam to put an intra-osseous cannula in her tibia when she heard Joe's voice and stuck her head out of the cubicle.

'Joe, have you got a minute?'

'For you, always,' he said softly. 'What's up?'

'Three-year-old girl, Lily, severe gastroenteritis, she's dehydrated and becoming slightly delirious and I cannot for the life of me find a vein I can get into. I found one and it's blown, Jenny's tried and failed—I don't think it's possible. Can you do an IO for me?'

'Let me have a look. Have you got a very fine cannula in case I can find a vein?'

'Yes, I've got a handful,' she said wryly, and took him in.

'Hi, I'm Joe,' he said to the parents, then crouched down to Lily's level. 'Hi, Lily. My name's Joe. Do you mind if I have a look at you, poppet?'

Her lip wobbled, and he smiled reassuringly.

'It's OK. Don't worry, sweetheart. You just lie there for a minute, I'm not going to hurt you.'

He turned her little hands over, checked the veins, moved down to her elbows, and smiled. 'Got one,' he said softly. 'Right, Lily, I'm going to rub some lovely magic cream on your arm, and then I'm going to put a funny little tube in it to give your body a drink, OK?'

Her lip wobbled again but her mother cuddled her and he smeared on a little local anaesthetic, chatted to them for a moment to give it time to work and then he put a soft tourniquet round her arm, gave the skin a little wipe to remove the cream and before Lily could protest, the line was in, taped down and ready to go.

They left Jenny setting it up and went out into the corridor.

'You're quite good at this vein-finding thing, aren't you?' Iona said with a little twinge of envy.

'You're only jealous,' he teased. 'And, yes, I am good at it but then I need to be. In another world I probably would have been a water diviner,' he added with a grin. 'So how's it going otherwise?'

'OK. Busy. How's the revision going?'

'Oh, don't. It's a nightmare. I'll never pass. There's just so much to know and my head feels as if it's going to burst, but hey. This time on Friday it'll all be over.'

'Are you back on Friday night?' she asked hopefully, but he shook his head.

'No, I won't be home until Sunday, probably early afternoon? I promised my parents I'd go and see them. I've been neglecting them, but I'll leave after breakfast. Stay the night on Sunday?' he added, in a murmur, and she felt a little surge of happiness.

'Yes, that'll be nice.'

'Nice?'

She felt herself colour. 'You know what I mean.'

'I do. I'll look forward to it,' he said softly, and grinning that mischievous grin he sauntered off and she went back to little Lily, trying to suppress her smile.

She shouldn't have done it.

She should have waited until after the weekend, but she hadn't been able to wait. And now there it was, the little white wand, saying 'Not Pregnant'.

Her period wasn't even due yet, not until Saturday, but the tests were good these days and she'd so hoped—

She bit her lips. She'd have to tell Joe, of course, when she saw him. She'd probably know by then for sure anyway, because her period would have started. And maybe he wouldn't want to see her, if she was out of action? Not much fun for him, and he hadn't had a lot of fun of any sort recently. And tomorrow was his exam.

She'd sent him a text wishing him luck, but she hadn't heard back. Too busy, probably.

She threw the wand in the bin, washed her hands and went back to work, but she felt sick. Pregnant sick? No. Really sick.

Little Lily's bug? She'd had gastroenteritis really badly and would have been shedding viruses all over the place, including on her.

She turned back to the cloakroom, lost her lunch and went home. No point in giving it to anyone else, she thought, but then after a few hours of slight stomach cramps, it all settled down again and she woke up on Friday morning still slightly queasy but feeling much better.

And then, against her better judgement and because she'd bought a two-pack, she did another pregnancy test.

Just in case.

Not Pregnant.

And still queasy. She phoned work, told them she still felt unwell and was advised to stay off for forty eight hours for staff and patient safety, so she tackled her laundry, tidied the flat—long overdue because it had been Libby's turn—changed the sheets and then dug out her notes on the course she'd done the previous week and did some extra study.

And then on Friday night she had a call from Joe.

'Hi. I'm on my way home. My mother's not feeling very well, she's got a horrible cold apparently so they've told me not to come. Fancy coming over? I'll be home in about an hour.'

She closed her eyes, relief flooding her, because she really, really needed him. 'That would be great.'

'Good. Pack a bag, come for the weekend.'

She opened her mouth to tell him, then changed her mind. 'OK. Ring me when you're back, I'll come straight over.'

She arrived fifteen minutes after he called, and he let her in, took one look at her and frowned. She looked pale, and definitely not her usual bouncy self.

'Hey, what's up?' he asked gently.

'I think I've had a touch of Lily's bug—that little girl? I was sick once and I've felt a bit queasy but nothing much.'

'Yeah, I've been feeling queasy, too. I reckon we've both had a touch of it, but I'm not surprised, she was shedding viruses all over us. Come on, come and sit down and have something to drink. You're probably dehydrated and that won't help the nausea. Electrolyte replacement?'

'Oh, no, it's disgusting. Can I smell toast? Because I'm suddenly ravenous, and tea and toast would be just amazing.'

He laughed. 'I'm glad that's what you fancy,

because all there is in the house is the remains of a stale loaf and some out of date milk, but it passed the sniff test. That do you?'

She chuckled. 'Sounds fine to me.'

He made them both tea while she buttered the toast, then they took it through to the sitting room and ate it on the sofa.

'So how was your exam?' she asked.

'Gruelling and very, very hard. I'm sure I will have failed. Still, I can resit.'

'You might have to have another go at getting me pregnant, as well,' she said, and put the toast down, her face crumpling.

Oh, no. He put his arm round her and hugged her gently against his side. 'Oh, sweetheart. When did you find out?'

'Today. I did a test. I know it's stupid of me, but I did it and it was negative.'

He frowned. 'Isn't it too early to tell?'

She shook her head. 'No. Apparently not, and I've done it twice now. Joe, what if I can't get pregnant? What if I'm like Isla? Then I'll never be able to give her a baby—'

Her face crumpled, and he drew her gently

into his arms and cradled her against his chest while she cried. It was so like her that her first thought had been for her sister, not for herself, and his heart ached for her.

'Hey,' he murmured, rocking her gently. 'Come on, it'll be all right.'

'But what if it isn't, Joe? What if I *can't* get pregnant? We're identical twins, so I guess it's possible we have the same body chemistry, if that's the problem, or the same anatomical issues—although she didn't have any, come to that, and—'

'Your period isn't due until tomorrow, is it?'

She shook her head.

'So don't borrow trouble. Pregnancy tests can be wrong. Maybe it's too early.'

'Or maybe I hadn't ovulated after all, maybe that happened later, too late. Or earlier. We only had one night.'

He sighed. 'I know, and that's my fault—'

'It's not your fault, you were busy. And you were pretty dedicated to the task on the Saturday night,' she added with a wobbly smile.

He could have hugged her for that. Well, for that and a whole host of other reasons that he'd rather not analyse, so he stuck the mug back in her hand instead. 'Here. Drink this and finish your toast, and then let's go to bed. I'm shattered, and you look as if you could do with a good night's sleep, too.'

She nodded, drank the tea, finished the toast and then closed her eyes. 'That's better. Thank you.'

'It's OK. Come on, bed for you.'

She wasn't going to argue.

He took her upstairs, undressed her, sent her into the bathroom first and then tucked her into bed.

'I'll be two minutes,' he said, and she snuggled down under his duvet, breathed in the scent of him on the sheets and sighed in disappointment. No scent of him. He must have changed the sheets.

For her? She smiled slightly at her silliness. Why would he do that for her? He was probably just fastidious.

Then he walked back in, stripped, turned off the light and got into bed beside her, folding her into his arms. 'OK?'

She breathed in the scent of him, rested her head on his chest and smiled. 'I am now,' she said softly, and drifted off to sleep in seconds.

CHAPTER SEVEN

SOMETHING WOKE HER.

A noise? It was utterly silent, apart from the soft sound of Joe breathing by her side, but then it came again, a short, sharp bark, and he swore under his breath and she laughed.

'It's not funny. I'm going to kill it one of these nights,' he growled, and she chuckled, knowing it was an empty threat.

'I can't see you as a hunter-gatherer type, somehow,' she murmured, and he rolled towards her, his mouth finding hers in the dark. He was still smiling. She could feel it in the shape of his lips, the creases round his eye as she laid her hand against his face.

But then the smile faded as his lips tasted hers, nibbling, tormenting, moving out along the line of her jaw to that ticklish place below her ear, his warm breath drifting over the skin and making her arch her neck to give him better access.

She felt his tongue flick her earlobe, then the cooling as he blew softly on it and then moved on, down, over her throat, pausing in the little hollow where her pulse was beating, to do the same again.

She felt his hands on her body, searching, smoothing, stroking, felt the soft sighs of his breath against her skin as he found something he liked—her hip, the curve of her bottom, the inside of her thigh.

And then he moved on, up over her ribs, cradling her breast with a warm, dry palm, his fingers teasing her nipple. His mouth found the other one, his tongue flicking, and she moaned and arched against him.

'Joe—'

'I'm here.'

'I know. I want…'

'Shh. All in good time.'

She threaded her fingers through his hair, her body writhing as he found endless ways to torment her with those wicked hands that seemed to understand her so well, the mouth that had no boundaries.

She tried to touch him, to reach down between

them but he stopped her, his hands taking hers and shackling them loosely above her head as his mouth claimed hers. His knee nudged her legs apart, his thigh moving rhythmically. She could feel the firm jut of his erection on her hip as he rocked against her, feel the pounding of his heart against her own, his breath faster now as he moved over her, freeing her hands at last to touch him as he sank into her and went still.

'Don't move,' he groaned, his body taut, his breath brushing her face as he fought for control, but she couldn't wait, couldn't lie still when she knew all he'd do was torment her more, and she was done with that. She rocked against him, her hands moving urgently down his back, finding his taut, firm buttocks and urging him closer, deeper, beyond reason now.

'Ah, dammit, Iona,' he hissed, half laughing, and then he started to move, thrusting deep into her, all humour gone now, totally focused on wringing every last drop of sensation out of their bodies. She felt her body rising to meet his, the coiled need inside her spiralling tighter and tighter until it shattered and she sobbed his name and took him with her into oblivion…

* * *

They spent the weekend together doing nothing but eating, sleeping and making love, and he taught her more about her body than she'd ever known existed.

They showered together, cooked together after his food order was delivered, played chess—he won, of course—and then went back to bed and did it all over again. And again.

And then, early on Sunday afternoon, he sent her home.

'I have to visit my aunt.'

She searched his eyes. 'Can I come?'

She saw humour there, as well as alarm. 'Absolutely not. Not after this weekend.'

'What's so special about this weekend? She won't know if we don't tell her.'

He laughed. 'You reckon? You've got stubble burn on your top lip, you look like the cat that got the cream and the woman's not stupid, so, no. She knows more about me than anyone else on earth, but there are some things that I won't tell even her, and this is one of them.' He was serious now, his voice dropping. 'I don't want her to know—not about this, not about us. She'd only start matchmaking and she's bad enough without encouragement, and neither of us are in this for the long haul, so—no. At least, not today, when a blind man could see what we've been doing. Maybe another time. Perhaps when you're pregnant.'

He kissed her again—to soften the blow? It wasn't a blow, not really, and she could see where he was coming from, but the word 'pregnant' had stopped her thoughts in their tracks.

'OK. You win,' she said, and gathering her things up, she kissed him goodbye, got into the car and drove to the nearest supermarket, picked up another pregnancy test and went home.

'Hello, darling! You're looking very chipper. What have you been up to?'

'Nothing,' he lied. 'I'm just glad the exam's over.'

'You didn't come yesterday.'

He just stopped the laugh. If she only knew...

'You weren't expecting me because I was supposed to be with my parents, and—anyway, I had things to do, so I thought I'd stick to what we'd arranged.'

'You're an appalling liar. It's Iona, isn't it? You spent the weekend with her.'

'No. I didn't.'

She just smiled. 'Such a pedant. All right, *she* spent the weekend with *you*. I hope you didn't set my house on fire.'

He closed his eyes, groaned in despair and gave up the unequal struggle. 'Look, it's nothing. It's not going to go anywhere, neither of us is looking for happy-ever-after, it's just a bit of fun, so don't get excited. It's not good for your heart.'

'On the contrary. Seeing you happily settled with a decent woman would be very good for my heart.'

'Well, it's not going to be Iona, and it's probably not going to be anyone ever, so you need to find another way to entertain yourself apart from meddling in my love life.'

'So it is love, then?'

Why was she so quick to pick up on the minutiae?

'It's just a euphemism, Elizabeth. And my *sex* life is none of your business. I am, as you pointed out very recently, a grown man. I am allowed my privacy. And, no, we did not set your house on fire,' he added wryly.

She just smiled, patted his knee as if he was five and sat back with a smug expression on her face. 'I knew it the moment I saw you. You look like the cat that got the cream. So how was the exam?'

His phone tinged as he got into the car, and he pulled it out of his pocket and opened the text.

It was from Iona, just one word.

Pregnant.

He stared at it, his emotions in freefall. It was happening. She was going to have a baby, and give it to Isla and Steve.

His baby.

He swallowed, dropped his head back against the head restraint and closed his eyes. *Not his baby. Not, not, not his baby.* Not hers, either, but a gift for Isla. Better remember that.

He started the car, drove home, walked into the house, shut himself in the study and worked until he couldn't see straight. Then, a little after midnight, he ate some toast, went up to bed and found a tangled mess that still carried the scent of her body. He breathed it in, his body roared to life and he stripped the bed, changed the sheets, had a shower and tried again.

Better—until he closed his eyes, and then the memories flooded back anyway. All the things he'd done to her, the things she'd done to him, the things they'd done together right here in his bed. And the shower. And the sitting room. The only room apart from two of the bedrooms that was free from memories was the study, but he'd spent enough time in there in the last two weeks to last him a lifetime, and he wasn't going back there now.

So he lay awake, in the bed where they'd—no. Not made love—had sex. Glorious, extensive, mind-blowing, all-consuming sex. Just as they'd done two weeks ago in the other room, the night he'd apparently made her pregnant.

And he missed her. Missed her body, but also her warmth, her mischievous sense of humour, her gentleness, her kindness.

He was not in love with her! And he wasn't going to be.

Ever.

* * *

He didn't reply.

Maybe he hadn't got her text. The signal in the village was a bit patchy. Maybe he was in the study and his phone couldn't pick up the signal there.

Or he didn't know what to say? Was she not meant to have told him?

She phoned Isla, who burst into tears at the news and made her cry as well, then she put the phone on hands free and Steve joined in, and eventually they stopped sniffing and asked questions. When was it due? How was she feeling?

'Early July—it's really, really early days, and you know, it might not happen,' she warned, trying not to let them build their hopes up, but she'd had to tell *someone*, and as Joe didn't seem interested, she'd done the next best thing.

They talked some more, and then Isla asked what Joe's reaction had been.

'I haven't spoken to him yet,' she said, not entirely untruthfully, and they seemed happy with that, which got her off the hook, but after she'd hung up she thought about work, about seeing him and maybe having to tell him there, in a public place.

Not that there was any urgency. As she'd told Isla and Steve, it was very early days, but—she wished he'd ring her. Just so she knew he knew, and was OK with it. Too late if he wasn't, but hey. He'd signed up for it, known exactly what he was doing because he'd done it before, for heaven's sake!

Only not like this. Not so intimately, or with so much passion and feeling.

Not in person.

Whatever, there was nothing either of them could do about it now, so there was no point worrying. And he might simply not have picked up the text.

Or decided that since they'd achieved their objective, his job was done and he could step back and forget her?

She had a shower and went to bed because there was nothing more she could do tonight. She'd talk to him tomorrow and get some answers, hopefully before she went crazy.

* * *

'Hi.'

She looked up from her coffee—decaf—and searched his eyes warily, not sure what she'd see there. Not a lot, for once. 'Did you get my text yesterday?'

He nodded but then looked away. 'Yes. I'm sorry I didn't reply, I was working. Mind if I sit down?'

She nearly laughed. After what they'd done at the weekend, he had to ask?

'Be my guest.'

He sat down on the other chair at the little table by the café window, stirred his coffee—black, no sugar, hence no need to stir—and then finally met her eyes again. 'So,' he said, his voice so soft she almost had to lipread. 'It happened.'

'Yes, it happened. Isla and Steve are delighted.'

'Good. Does it—change anything?'

Her heart thumped. 'In what way?'

'This...' he gestured between them '...whatever it is.'

'I don't know. I hope not. Not as far as I'm concerned, anyway. One is a—business arrangement. The other, this friends-with-benefits thing—'

'Is strictly pleasure,' he murmured, his voice low and laden with meaning, his eyes smouldering now and easy to read. A smile touched them. 'Good. I was hoping you'd say that.'

She smiled back, feeling her body flood with relief because when he hadn't replied she hadn't known what to think, and she'd been so afraid that she'd lost him. 'Yes. Thank you for the weekend, by the way. It was...' She couldn't find a word to sum it up, so she just shrugged and smiled again.

'Yes, it was, wasn't it?' he said, his answering smile flickering behind the fire in his eyes and telling her everything she needed to know.

'So how was your aunt?' she asked, scrabbling for her sanity.

He rolled his eyes and groaned. 'She took one look at me and knew. I denied it, but apparently I'm a useless liar.'

'You are.'

He grinned at that. 'Well, it takes one to know one.'

He picked up her glass of water, put a splash

of it in his coffee and drained it, then got to his feet. 'Gotta go. Stuff to do.'

'Isn't there always. So—will you call me?'

He nodded. 'Of course. You know where I am in the meantime, if you need me for anything. I meant what I said.'

His eyes were serious now, and she nodded.

'I know. Thank you—for that and for everything. I'm so grateful.' Grateful for what he'd given her—well, Isla and Steve, really—and grateful for his promise to stand by her, even more so because it had been unsolicited. That, more than anything, spoke volumes about him, and as she watched him walk away, she thought what a shame it was that she'd met him after Natalie had destroyed his trust and—how had he put it? Taken his innocence and burned it alive before his eyes? Something like that. Powerful image, and one she could easily identify with. Dan had done much the same to her.

She picked up her cup, took a sip of the tepid coffee and put it down, drank the water instead and headed back to work. She'd slipped out in a quiet moment, but no doubt that had all gone haywire by now. Time to get back to the real world.

* * *

Their 'friends with benefits' arrangement, as she'd described it, worked well for the next few weeks.

He didn't ask her to move in, she didn't suggest it. Sometimes she stayed over, sometimes she didn't, and when morning sickness hit—why morning, when it was all day, every day?—she stayed in her flat when she wasn't working and slept and ate carbs like they were going out of fashion.

It was short-lived, and by the time she was ten weeks pregnant, she was starting to feel better, and so instead of hiding out and feeling sorry for herself, whenever they were both free their evenings and weekends were spent curled up in front of the wood burner in the sitting room, reading and talking and binge-watching box sets on catch-up TV.

It was blissful, but a little bit of her had to keep reminding herself that they were only playing happy families and it wasn't for real.

She went home to her parents' for Christmas with Isla and Steve, and on Christmas morning they told their parents that she was pregnant with their baby. Her mother cried. Her father patted her shoulder and frowned, but either way, hers or Isla's, they were going to have a second grandchild. Johnnie and Kate were in Geneva with her parents, but they made a video call and broke the news, and Johnnie was speechless for a moment.

'Wow,' he said after a long pause. 'That's mega, Iona. Are you OK?'

She smiled at him, her little brother worrying about her. 'Yes, I'm fine, it's all good. How are you?'

They chatted for a bit, then she left their parents to speak to him and took herself off to the kitchen to raid the fridge.

'Hey, we're eating soon,' Isla said, following her into the kitchen, but she just laughed.

'Not soon enough. I am seriously short of carbs and I'm not waiting until the Aga's decided it's warmed up enough to finish the turkey. I've been here before.'

She found the remains of last night's rice pudding and hauled it out. Her mother made the most amazing rice pudding. Only Steve's presence prevented her from sticking her face in the dish and licking it out. She scraped up the last bit, put the enamelled pan on the floor for the dogs to lick and sat back.

'So, I have my twelve-week scan appointment at ten on Wednesday. Can you come?'

Isla sat forward, her face filled with longing. 'Can we?'

'Well, yes, of course. I was expecting you would.'

'Won't you be back at work?'

She nodded. 'Yes, but I'll have time off for the scan.'

And she'd have to tell James, she realised. Or HR. Both, probably. Whether she did or not, it'd be all round the hospital in a flash if she was spotted in the waiting room.

Her phone rang, and she pulled it out of her jeans—new, with stretch to accommodate the carbs—and it was Joe. 'Sorry, I need to take this,' she told them, and went out into the study. 'Hi. Happy Christmas.'

'Happy Christmas. How's it going?'

'OK. We told them. Mum got a bit teary, Dad was just Dad, and Johnnie was shocked, but all in all, OK. How's work?'

'Busy, but not too bad so far. When are you back?'

'I'm working tomorrow night, so I'll leave after breakfast and sleep when I get back, if I can. Then I'm off on Tuesday, the normal rota Wednesday onwards.'

Except for the scan, which she didn't mention. She'd rather do that face to face.

'That's a shame. I'm working tomorrow and Tuesday, so I won't see you until Tuesday evening, if then. Depends when I get away. Oh, I had a great Christmas present, by the way. I passed my exam.'

'Seriously? Well done, you. I thought you were convinced you'd failed?'

'I was. Apparently they set the bar low.'

'Did they say that?'

'No, of course not, but *I* wouldn't have passed me if I'd done the examining.'

She laughed at him. 'You're so hard on yourself. So—maybe see you on Tuesday evening?'

'Yes, hopefully, if I get off in time. Drive carefully.'

'Anybody would think you cared.'

'I do. I don't want to end up embolising your

mangled blood vessels after they pick you out of the wreckage,' he said candidly, but there was an underlying thread of what sounded very like affection, and she chuckled.

'I'll try not to ruin your day.'

'ED trauma call, ten minutes.'

Really? She'd been at work eleven hours, and this was the fifth call in the last two. What was wrong with everyone? Why weren't they asleep in their beds at six in the morning?

She went to the desk. 'Do you want me to take this?'

'If you could, please. Elderly lady in a care home. She's had a fall, query fractured neck of femur. Elizabeth Williamson, aged eighty four. I'll get her notes up.'

'Thank you,' she murmured, her mind working. Elizabeth, care home, eighties—and then the ambulance arrived and she was wheeled in and Iona knew without looking at the notes. The paramedic did the handover, and she waited until he'd gone and introduced herself with a smile.

'Hello, my name's Iona, I'm a doctor and I'm going to be looking after you today.'

'So, I finally get to meet the mystery woman,' she murmured, so quietly that only Iona heard. She smiled warmly, a mischievous twinkle in the eyes so like his. 'I'm Joseph's aunt, Elizabeth.' She held out her frail hand, and Iona took it gently.

'I know. The eyes are a bit of a giveaway,' she said with a wry smile. 'I'm very pleased to meet you, too. I've heard so much about you.'

'Oh, dear. I interfere, so I'm sure none of it was good.'

She laughed at that. 'It was. He's very, very fond of you.' She turned to the nurse who was with her, hoping she hadn't heard the conversation. 'Could you please call Dr Baker and tell him his aunt's here?'

'Oh, do you really need to, Iona? He'll only lecture me.'

'I'm sure you can take it. So what happened, then, Dr Williamson? Did you fall?'

'Elizabeth. And, yes, I was in the bathroom, and I just—well, to be honest, I think I must have passed out. I have postural hypotension, so it's quite likely.'

'And how long were you there before you had help?'

'I don't know. Quite a while. Two or three hours?'

She frowned. That was a long time to be on the floor alone. 'OK, let's try and get to the bottom of this, then. Can we get a monitor on please, and do a twelve-lead ECG, and we'll take some blood. You might be a bit anaemic or have an infection.' She reeled off a list for the bloods, turned back to Elizabeth and smiled. 'I think we'll wait for Joe before we order any X-rays. He's bound to have an opinion. I take it you're happy for me to share your medical details with him?'

'Of course. He'd only get it out of me anyway, so you might as well tell him.' She tilted her head on one side. 'You're a very lovely young woman, Iona,' she murmured softly. 'I wish Joe wasn't so set on self-destruct. He could do a lot worse than you—has done, of course, with that dreadful Natalie woman. I wish he'd met you first. You've put a twinkle in his eye and a spring in his step I haven't seen in years.'

'Well, that's as maybe, but we probably

shouldn't be talking about him here,' she said with a wry smile. 'Do you mind if I have a look at you, Elizabeth?'

'No, of course I don't. I know you have to do your job.'

She was a mass of bruises. There was a bruise forming already on the point of her hip, where she'd gone down, and she had several others, which was a bit worrying.

'Do you always bruise so easily?' she asked, covering her again, and Elizabeth shrugged.

'Only if I fall.'

'And do you fall often?'

Her smile was wise and tired. 'More often than I should. I feel very tired these days.'

'Well, we'll check all that while we've got you here— Oh, look who it is. That was quick.'

'I was here, the home phoned me. What on earth have you done to yourself?' he asked fondly, stooping to kiss his aunt.

'I fell in the bathroom.'

'Oh, that's such a cliché. I would have expected something a little bit more imaginative from you. So, any injuries?' he asked, turning to Iona, and she could see the worry in his eyes.

'Query neck of femur,' Iona told him. 'Bruising over the left trochanter consistent with a fall on her side, other bruising on the same side and also some older bruising elsewhere. I've ordered a whole raft of bloods, but I haven't ordered any X-rays yet because I know you'll have a better idea than me of what you want.'

He tried to smile. 'You must have read my mind. OK, Elizabeth, can you put any weight on that leg?'

'I haven't tried, but possibly not. It's quite sore.'

'Right, let's get a CT of the pelvis, just in case. I don't want to miss anything, I'd never hear the end of it.'

The CT was clear, to everyone's relief, but the bloods showed she was anaemic. Iona stayed with her past the end of her shift because Joe had to leave, but he came back and she told him about the other falls, out of earshot.

'She hasn't told me about this.'

'No. I'm sure she hasn't. She may not have told the home. I spoke briefly to the lady who came in with her, but she's gone back to the home now. Maybe you need to call them.'

He nodded. 'So what's the plan?'

'They're putting her in a side ward while the geriatrician has a look at the bloods, then he's going to work out what to do and call you. I gave him your number, and he knows you're here.'

'Good. Thank you. Now you need to go home and get some sleep. I'm sure your shift ended ages ago.'

She nodded. 'OK.' She hesitated a moment, then added quietly, 'Isla and Steve are coming down tomorrow morning. I've got my first scan at ten. Do you want to come?'

He shook his head. 'No. Of course not, it's nothing to do with me.'

She smiled her understanding. 'I thought so, but I wanted you to have the option. So I'll see you whenever, then. Probably not tonight if she's kept in.'

He gave a rueful smile. 'Probably not. I hope it all goes well tomorrow. Thanks for looking after Elizabeth.'

The scan was incredible.

She'd seen hundreds of scan photos when she'd done her obstetrics rotation, but this was *her* baby. *Hers and Joe's, so small, so perfect, so incredible. Her baby—*

'Oh, Steve, it's beautiful—look at that little nose!' Isla said, her voice cutting through the dream and turning it to dust.

No. Not her baby, and not Joe's. It was Isla's baby, Isla and Steve's.

She swallowed, turned her face away from the screen and willed it all to be over.

'There we are, all done and it's all looking good. Do you want a photo?'

'Yes—oh, yes, please,' Isla said, and then asked for two.

They went out to collect them from the reception desk, and she straightened her clothes, got off the couch and met the sonographer's curious eyes.

'I'm a surrogate for them. She's my twin sister, so it's sort of her baby.'

She nodded, the curiosity turning to sympathy. 'Take care,' she said gently, and Iona tried to smile, gave up and walked out.

'Here—your photo. Thank you so much for letting us come. That was just amazing.'

She stared at the square white envelope, didn't

quite know what to do with it but took it anyway. 'Thanks. And you're welcome. Right, I need to get back to work. Love you lots.'

She hugged them both and walked away, suddenly conscious of the tiny life growing inside her, and her need to protect it. She'd been dodging Resus recently because of the X-rays, and she knew it was time to tell James.

Not that she had a choice, now, because she hadn't taken her bag and had nowhere to put the envelope, so when she got back and ran into James and Sam in the locker room, they took one look at the envelope, familiar from scans of their own small children, and Sam made an excuse to leave, closing the door behind him.

'Yes,' she said to James, without waiting for his question. 'I'm having a baby—for my sister. It's due on the eighth of July, and I'll work as long as I can, hopefully to my due date, then I'll be back two weeks afterwards.'

James stared at her, slightly open-mouthed, and then shut his mouth, waited until she'd put the envelope in her locker and then ushered her to his office and sat her down.

'Iona, I don't really know what to say.'

She laughed softly. 'You don't have to say any-thing, James. I don't want any special conces-sions, I don't want a fuss made, and I'd rather nobody knew about it until they have to.'

'I don't think it's a secret. You've been looking peaky, said you weren't feeling well and mak-ing excuses not to work in Resus. It's not that, it's what you said about your sister. So is this an implanted embryo?'

She could have lied, could have said yes, but he'd been so good with her from day one she couldn't bring herself to do it, so she told him the severely edited truth. 'And I'm not going to take any annual leave,' she added, 'so you won't be short-staffed.'

'I don't care about that, I care about you. If there's anything you need, anything you want, time off without notice, anything—just ask me, OK? And you will take annual leave, and as much maternity leave as you need to. I don't want you getting stressed and exhausted.'

'I don't want any concessions—'

'Tough. And if anyone gives you a hard time, refer them to me.' He stood up, came round the desk, pulled her gently to her feet and gave her a little hug. 'I always knew you were a kind and generous person. I didn't realise you were this brave. For what it's worth, I think what you're doing for your sister is amazing. Now go and find something safe to do, and remember, my door's always open.'

She felt her eyes fill, blinked hard and nodded. 'Thank you.'

He wasted every free minute of the day wondering how the scan had gone, if she'd been all right, how she was dealing with it. She came over in the evening after he'd called her to say he was home, and she walked in and handed him an envelope.

'Here,' she said. 'Just in case you wanted to see it.'

He held it in his fingers like an unexploded bomb, staring at it in horrified fascination. 'How did it go?'

'Fine. Everything looks good. It's due on the eighth of July.'

He dropped the envelope on the hall table like a hot brick and went into the kitchen, desperate to change the subject. 'I made a curry.'

'Not turkey, I hope.'

'No. Not turkey. It's venison.'

'You didn't shoot it!'

He laughed and pulled her into his arms, relenting. 'No, of course I didn't shoot it. I don't have a gun and, anyway, I don't particularly like venison. It's a Goan fish curry, very mild, so it shouldn't give you acid reflux.'

He bent his head and kissed her lingeringly, then let her go, laid the table and dished up.

'I saw James,' she told him. 'He'd worked out weeks ago that I'm pregnant because I was avoiding Resus because of the radiation risk, but I explained the situation and he was brilliant about it.'

He froze. 'Did you tell him I was the donor?' he asked, and she looked horrified.

'No, of course not! I won't tell anyone that. It's nobody's business but ours. This curry's lovely, by the way. Thank you. How's your aunt doing?'

'OK. She's back in the home, on iron supplements. They're going to monitor her. It might be gastric erosion from painkillers, so they've switched her to something gentler on the stomach and put her on omeprazole. She's not happy. She says the painkillers are useless.'

They chatted more about her, then about his plans for the kitchen, his work schedule, but he wasn't really concentrating because out of the corner of his eye he could see the envelope sitting on the hall table, and he didn't know what to do with it.

He should have thrown it out. Should have done something with it—lit the fire with it, anything—because on New Year's Day he took Elizabeth home for a festive lunch, turned his back to hang up their coats, and the first thing she did was pick it up.

'You haven't opened your card,' she said, and before he could stop her she'd opened the envelope and pulled it out.

'Don't—'

But he was too late. She opened the card, saw the grainy ultrasound photo and gasped softly. 'Joe?'

'Do you have no boundaries?' he asked, snatching it out of her hand and stuffing it back in the envelope without looking at it, and she put her hand over her mouth and her eyes filled.

'It's Iona's, isn't it?' she asked, ignoring his comment.

'No. It's her sister's.'

'But the name said Iona—'

'It's her sister's baby,' he said firmly. 'She's not keeping it.'

'And yours.'

'No!' he denied, and then softened. 'No. It's not *my* baby, Elizabeth, it's not *her* baby, either, and it's definitely not *our* baby. She's having it for Isla, so don't get any ideas and start knitting, because it's not going to happen.'

'Oh, Joseph,' she murmured sadly, and took his hand, a tear trickling down her cheek. 'Dear boy—'

He retrieved his hand. 'I'm not a boy, Elizabeth. I'm a man, and I know my own mind, and I can make decisions for myself. And this was my decision, to do this for her, for them. So don't waste sympathy on me, because I'm fine with it, so's Iona. It's all good.'

'Is it? Then why are you so angry?'

He had no answer for that, at least not one he

was prepared to voice, so he led her through to the kitchen, parked her at the table and put the vegetables on to steam while he made the gravy and tried to get his emotions under control.

CHAPTER EIGHT

THE WEATHER CHANGED, growing much colder as winter got into its stride, and Iona thought she felt a cooling in Joe, as well.

The roads were icy, he didn't want her risking an accident, and anyway he had work to do, another course to go on, another exam coming up…

Excuses? It felt like it, but then out of the blue he'd pick her up, take her home, feed her, make love to her as if she was the most precious thing in the world, and then return her to her flat. Even then, he seemed distracted. The only emotion she felt from him was when they were making love, and otherwise he seemed to be trying to distance himself from her.

Or from the baby?

No. She didn't think so, because when he made love to her, he'd caress her bump, lay kisses on it. Was that the action of a man who was trying to distance himself from it? Not that he could avoid it. She was noticeably pregnant now, the small bump above her pelvis appearing at fourteen weeks and continuing to grow. Her waist thickened, her breasts grew heavier, and her scrubs were barely hiding it.

Maybe he was genuinely busy, and concerned for her on the icy roads? She didn't know, but she needed to, so the next time he phoned and asked if she was free, she drove over to his house an hour earlier than planned and found the house in darkness.

Stupid. He might be anywhere, expecting to pick her up on his way home. Or maybe he was in his study. She rang the doorbell, and the hall light came on and he opened the door.

'Iona? I thought I was picking you up?'

'You were. I thought I'd save you the job.' She went in without waiting for him to ask, and turned to him, meeting his puzzled eyes with determination.

'Is this some kind of test?' she asked him bluntly.

He frowned. 'Test? Is what a test? I don't understand.'

'Leaving me in suspense from day to day, picking me up when it suits you, then dropping me again until the next time you can fit me into your schedule? Is it because you're bored with me, or is it to see if I get bored like Natalie—?'

'No! Iona, no, absolutely not! You're nothing like her and I'm not in the slightest bit bored with you!' He took her hands, unknotting them from each other and wrapping them tightly in his. 'I just need to work and, believe me, I'd far rather not. And it's not that I don't want to see you. I do. I just can't concentrate if you're here, and I *have* to.'

'Why? Why push yourself so hard if you don't want to?'

'Because there's...' He hesitated, clearly torn, then met her eyes again. 'There's a consultancy in the offing, totally unofficial and it may not happen, but my boss wants me for it, and I can't blow this because I want it, too. I want it—need it—so badly I can taste it, but if you're here I know I won't work because I'll want to be with you, I'll get distracted, and I can't afford to let that happen, not now, not with so much at stake, but that doesn't mean I don't want you. You must know how much I want you, God knows, I can't disguise it, but I have to pass these exams if I'm going to stand a chance of the consultancy if it comes up.'

She felt stupid. Needy, whinging, pathetic—

'I'm sorry. I didn't realise the pressure you were under. Of course you have to work. I'll go—'

'No! No, stay. I was nearly done. Make yourself a drink, let me just finish off what I was doing and then I'll stop.'

'Are you sure?'

He pulled her into his arms and kissed her lingeringly, then let her go, strode down the hall to the study, turned off the light and came back. 'I'm sure. I'm done. It'll still be there tomorrow. Come in the sitting room and talk to me about anything you like except medicine.'

They didn't talk. Not for long. She ended up lying in his arms on the sofa while he kissed her tenderly, his fingers sifting through her hair. 'I've missed you,' she said, and he kissed her again.

'I've missed you, too. The only thing that's

getting me through the work is knowing you're there when I come up for air.'

'Which isn't often enough.' She stroked his face. 'You sound exhausted, Joe.'

'I am. I could sleep for a week, but there'll be time for that in the summer, when it's all over.'

It? The work—or the baby? Because by mid-summer, the baby would be Isla's... She sucked in a breath. 'So—tell me about this consultancy. Is it a new post?'

He nodded. 'They're trying to get funding. They've raised nearly all the money for the new angio-surgical suite, and my boss is going to be running it, which leaves the IR suite a bit in the lurch.'

'Hence the job.'

'Hence the job. So I need to make sure I'm ready for it. It could be my only chance to work here for years, by which time Elizabeth won't be here any longer and I will have missed my opportunity to spend time with her. And I owe her that time, for all she's done for me.'

She smiled, just so he knew she was teasing. 'So does she see you more than I do?'

He laughed a little ruefully. 'She does, but

not for long, and she's *much* less distracting,' he added, trailing a fingertip down her throat and under the V of her jumper to linger tantalisingly in her cleavage.

'What about your parents?' she asked, retrieving his hand. 'Don't you owe them?'

He sighed. 'I guess, but they're younger, they've got each other, so there's time for them later. And this...' He shifted, dropped a slow, lingering kiss in her cleavage and disentangled himself from her. 'I need to go and cook. Or we could go to the pub.'

'Or I could cook and you could go and finish whatever you were doing.'

He searched her eyes. 'Don't you mind?' he asked, and she had to laugh.

'No, silly. I don't mind at all. Go and do it, and I'll investigate the fridge.'

It set a new pattern, one in which she took care of him instead of the other way round. She kept out of his way for most of the week and then when it fitted with their shifts, she went to him, taking food already prepared so he didn't have to do it, and they spent the night together, talk-ing, eating, making love.

And then one day in February, she felt some-thing—a tiny flutter? It could have been anything, a movement of her gut, a muscle twitch—but then the next day she felt it again, stronger, so that if she laid her hand over it, she could feel the faintest movement under her palm.

Her baby was moving.

She felt a surge of joy, and then reined it back. Not her baby, Isla's baby. And in less than two weeks, they'd be coming down for the twenty-week anomaly scan.

Except they didn't. Isla had had been ill with a tummy bug in early January, and she phoned the day before the scan and said she still wasn't right and couldn't face the long journey from Northampton to Yoxburgh, so she'd made an appointment to see the doctor.

'You should have told me you were still ill,' she told Isla with a pang of guilt. 'It's been weeks since that bug, you shouldn't still be feeling funny, so I'm glad you're getting it checked out.'

'But I'll miss the scan, and I was so excited. I'm really sorry.'

'Don't be sorry. You take care, let me know what they say, and don't worry about not being here, it doesn't matter. I'll get you photos. You just get well.'

She put the phone down and smoothed her hand absently over her bump. It was a shame they couldn't make it, but the most important thing was that Isla went to the doctor and found out what was wrong.

She thought of all the things it could be. Hepatitis of some sort? Pancreatitis? A food intolerance, like dairy? That could happen after a tummy bug, so when she got to Joe's that evening she ran it by him.

'That's unusual,' he said, frowning slightly. 'Did you tell her to get it checked out?'

'She's already got an appointment with the doctor. Joe, what if something's really wrong?'

'It won't be. Lots of gastric bugs can trash you for weeks,' he said firmly, wrapping his arms round her and holding her close, rocking her against his chest. 'It'll be something simple like a lactose intolerance after the bug. Don't worry.'

'I know you're right, but I can't help worrying.

And they're going to miss the scan. She sounded gutted about that.'

'Do you need me to come with you?' he said after a beat.

Need? Or want? He sounded reluctant, and as far as she knew he hadn't even looked at the first scan photo. The envelope was still lying on the hall table, gathering dust.

'No, I'll be fine—unless you want to come? You're welcome.'

Very welcome, and for a second she thought he hesitated, but then he shook his head and she knew she'd imagined it.

'No, I'll be busy, you know what it's like. There's a lot of elective stuff tomorrow, as well, so it'll be like a production line. What time is it?'

'Ten thirty.'

'No. That's right in the middle of it. Sorry.'

Was that a tinge of regret in his voice? Could be. Or just her imagination. She buried her needy side and moved out of his arms, smiling up at him as she cradled his jaw and went up on tiptoe to kiss him. 'Don't worry. So, what's for supper? I'm ravenous.'

* * *

He spent all day trying not to think about Iona and her scan, but the day was hell on wheels as he'd expected and of course nothing was easy, things went wrong—one patient arrested, another had such tight kinks in the radial artery he had to start again using the femoral artery, someone else reacted to the contrast medium and almost died—and just when he thought it couldn't get any worse, he had a call from Iona and her voice sounded odd.

'Are you going to be long?'

'No. I'm done—why?'

'We need to talk. Can you come to mine?'

His heart thudded against his chest. Was it Isla? The baby? 'I'm on my way.' He ran to his car, drove to hers and rang the doorbell, and she came straight down, her face ashen.

'Right, let's get you home,' he said, slinging an arm around her and holding her close, and he led her to his car, drove her home, took her into the kitchen and sat her down. 'Right, talk to me, Iona. Tell me what's wrong. Is it the baby? Did they find something on the scan?'

She closed her eyes briefly, shook her head, and his heart speeded up.

'Is it Isla, then? Have they found something?'

She nodded, and gave what could have been a strangled laugh, but it was more of a sob.

'She's...' Her voice trailed off, but then she tried again. 'She's pregnant.'

The blood drained from his head. *'What?'*

'I know. I've spent all day convincing myself she's got something awful, and it turns out she's pregnant, and I don't know whether to laugh or cry.'

He stared at her, stunned. 'That's impossible. I don't understand. How can she be pregnant?'

Iona shrugged. 'I don't know, but apparently she is.'

He stood up, his legs shaking, and put the kettle on, stuck a carton of soup in the microwave while the kettle boiled, and then made them tea, plonking it down on the table in front of her and dropping back into his chair.

'So, what exactly did she say?'

She ignored the tea, using it as a hand warmer instead. 'She's thirteen weeks, give or take. She had no idea. She had a period, a bit light, a bit late, which she thought was odd, and then she got this horrible gastric bug which she thought was definitely a bug because she had diarrhoea, too, but she didn't get better. And she started to worry, so she went to the doctor today, which is why she couldn't come down, and it was a locum who'd never seen her and didn't know her history, and she said she thought it sounded as if she was pregnant, sent her off to produce a urine sample and it tested positive, but she couldn't hear a heartbeat so because of her history they thought it might be a molar pregnancy and sent her straight to hospital for a scan, and they found a perfectly normal thirteen-week foetus. So she rang me,' she ended, finally coming to a halt and taking a breath.

'So—what happens now? With...' *No, not our.* 'With this baby?'

Her eyes looked dazed. 'I don't know. We didn't talk about our baby, just hers, but she said she didn't know how to tell me. They'd only just found out, and she was a bit stunned. And of course there's no guarantee their baby will survive. She had a miscarriage years ago, with Steve, but nothing since and they've been trying everything for the last five years, so this is completely unexpected and she's convinced she'll lose it, but—what if she doesn't lose it, Joe?

'What if she goes to term and they don't want our baby? I mean, I know it sounds selfish and obviously I don't want them to lose it, that would be tragic, and I'm overjoyed for them, but neither of us signed up for this. I can't have a baby now, not at this stage in my career. And on the other hand, if they lose theirs and then still want ours, will they be able to love her? Will she be as precious, as loved, as the baby they lost? I don't think so, and I couldn't bear that, and I don't know what to do—'

'There's nothing you need to do,' he said, his heart pounding, because this was his worst nightmare come true, the fact that things had changed when she was already pregnant, and now there was no way back. 'You don't know what's going to happen, whether she's going to lose it or not, but even if they do lose their baby and have this one as planned, it will be precious and of course they'll love it.'

Except there was no 'of course' about it. Yes, they'd love it, but—as much as their own? No.

How could they? Would they say they wanted it just as an insurance policy, in case their own baby died? That wasn't why he'd agreed to this, to give Isla and Steve a backup baby! There was no way back, no way out of it, and he had to remind himself it wasn't his mess. Iona was pregnant, she was having a baby for her sister, and his only role in this was support for her. How they'd sort it all between them wasn't his business.

Unless they changed their minds and left Iona literally holding the baby.

Did that make it his business? Did the fact that his baby might not be loved and cherished as it surely deserved—did *that* make it his business? Should he—*could* he—try and make a go of it with Iona? Because for all his denial, this *was* his baby. His own flesh and blood. His...

He filtered the conversation through his head again, and found what he was looking for. 'Did you say "she"?'

She looked up and met his eyes, and they welled with tears. 'Yes. It's a girl,' she said with a hitch in her voice, her free hand curling protectively over her bump. 'Our baby's a girl.'

A girl, a tiny little girl, who might end up with parents who did love her, but not quite as much as they would their own baby. Not nearly as much as he would...

Tears stinging his eyes, he got to his feet, walked to the other end of the kitchen and poured out the soup on autopilot.

'Here. You need to eat this. I'll butter some bread.'

'I don't want it—'

'Tough. You need to eat and so do I. Come on.'

She sat up straighter, arching her back a little as if it was aching, and he stared at the smooth, rounded curve of her abdomen. Their baby was in there. Their daughter...

He sat down abruptly at the table, cajoled Iona into eating, and then when she was done he led her upstairs, tucked her up in bed and headed for the shower.

The water was steaming hot, sluicing over him in a torrent, and he stood under it and let it wash away all the things that didn't matter. By the time he turned it off, the only thing left in his mind was Iona, and she needed him now as she'd never needed him before. The rest he could deal with when he knew what he was dealing with.

He towelled himself roughly dry, gave his hair another rub and got into bed behind her, wrapping himself around her and holding her close. She turned in his arms and he realised she was crying, and it made his chest ache with sadness.

He stroked her hair soothingly, pressing his lips to her wet face. 'It's all right, Iona, I'm here, I've got you, I'm going nowhere. It'll be OK,' he murmured, and he didn't know who he was trying to reassure—her, or himself...

She'd hoped the morning would bring clarity, but it didn't. It brought more worry, more stress, more uncertainty.

And a million 'what ifs'.

'It'll be OK,' he said again, after she'd poured out all her fears and worries all over him in a torrent. 'Just give it time. It'll work itself out.'

His hand cradled her cheek, his mouth finding hers, tenderly at first and then hungrily as she responded. His hand left her face, traced her body, his leg easing between hers as he stroked the taut skin over their baby. And then she felt a movement, and he froze.

'Was that—?'

She nodded, smiling wistfully. 'Yes. I felt it a week or two ago. She's a wriggler.'

'She is,' he said softly, his hand splayed over her bump. He shifted, his breath teasing over her skin as he bent and touched his lips to the place where his hand had been. 'Hello, you,' he murmured, and he sounded odd.

Awestruck?

Maybe. That was how she'd felt, but then she'd always been more ready for this than him. Until now, when she had no idea how it was going to end—

His mouth came back to hers, picking up where he'd left off, but his touch was gentler, more tender. More loving?

He had to start work before her, so he dropped her off at home en route to the hospital, parked the car and went to IR via the Park Café to pick up breakfast. A cappuccino with an extra shot, an almond croissant, and a banana, to redress the balance.

And while he was walking, he gave himself a stiff talking to. OK, so the baby had kicked and he'd felt it. So? Babies kicked. Any woman who'd ever been pregnant would tell you that. It didn't change anything. It still wasn't his baby, it didn't matter what Isla and Steve did, or what Iona did, come to that. She'd cope. Women did. She'd give her baby up to them, or she'd put her in child care, and go to work, and he'd press on with his life plan. Just a few more months down the line and it would all be over, for him at least, because it wasn't and never had been on his agenda for him to have a family at this point in his life and he wasn't going to be swayed by this sudden kink in life's direction.

Except that he wanted to see it—her. To maintain contact with her, follow her progress, maybe sometimes go to a Nativity play or school sports or something like that.

Things a father would do, he realised with a shock. Things he'd wanted to do for his other children, things he'd been denied, both by the donor process and then by Natalie.

So—did he want to be a father? Was that it?

Absolutely not. He'd get these exams out of

the way, finish his training and hopefully get the consultancy. Failing that, he'd look elsewhere.

And the baby, whoever she ended up being parented by, would be loved, he was sure of that. It just wouldn't be him because, apart from any other consideration, he'd given up that right. And he was shocked at how much it hurt…

CHAPTER NINE

JOE WAS WORKING AGAIN.

Well, still working, really, but the pace seemed to have picked up again. He worked gruelling hours in the hospital as it was, never clocked off on time, and then would go home and work until he couldn't see straight.

Not that he told her this, but she'd seen enough of the pattern, and so she left him to it because she realised how important it was to him that he should succeed. And not just for himself, but so that he could stay near Elizabeth for what time she had left.

If he was simply being driven by that urge to succeed, she would have found it harder to accept, but she knew he wasn't, so she left him alone rather than unloading all her angst on him when he really, really didn't need it.

This was between her and Isla, who still hadn't said what their plans were. March came and

went, then April, with the safe arrival of Johnnie
and Kate's baby boy, and then in the first week
of May Isla phoned her in the middle of her shift
to say she'd had a bleed—nothing drastic, but
it had triggered more scans, further tests, and
Iona knew they were worried something might
be wrong and they might lose it. And they still
hadn't said what they wanted to do about her
baby. They probably hadn't given it any more
thought, not yet, not when their own baby's life
seemed to hang in the balance.

And Iona found herself willing their little baby
to stay safe, to be fine, because that would mean
they wouldn't want *her* baby. Which was silly.
So silly, because how could she give her anything like the life that they would do? She'd be
on her own—how could she ask Joe to help her?
That wasn't fair, not what he'd signed up for.
And he'd made his attitude to relationships perfectly clear on many occasions.

'Take care,' she said gently. 'And keep in touch,
Isla. Let me know how you are. Love you.'

'Love you, too. Iona? Pray for us.'

Pray for them? She hadn't prayed in years, yet

she found herself doing it over and over again, a kind of mantra.

Please let it be all right. Please don't let them lose the baby. Please let it be—

'Iona?'

She looked up, blinking away tears, and James steered her into his office and shut the door.

'What's up?'

So she told him, all of it except the bit about Joe, and he listened in silence and then shook his head slowly.

'That's a lot to deal with. Do you need time off?'

'To do what? Sit at home and fret? No, absolutely not. I want to be busy. I don't want to have time to think, because it's pointless until I know what's happening.'

'If it all goes well and they don't want it—'

'Then I'll keep it, which is unfair on the baby, and career suicide, but what else can I do? I can't give her up for adoption, James—'

Her eyes welled, and she swiped the tears away angrily.

Don't cry! Don't give in!

'No, of course you can't, I can see that, but you'll cope, Iona. Women have always coped with this, even chosen it. There are ways, and I'll do everything I can to support you if it comes to that. Starting with you having a year off for maternity leave.'

'But—that would leave you in the lurch, and what do I do then? After a year? What do I do, James? It's not like I can take a staff grade, I'm not qualified.'

'Go into general practice? At least you'd get regular hours and you've worked in all the right fields. Just bear it in mind, and in the meantime go and have a lunch break and come back when you're ready.'

She wanted to hug him, but she made do with a wordless nod of thanks, and went to the Park Café, grabbing a decaf coffee and a sandwich and taking them out in the park.

She'd never thought of being a GP, but—could she? And keep her baby? She felt a leap of hope, and then squashed it, because she still hadn't heard from Isla and it might all change again in an instant.

* * *

There was a boy, he couldn't have been more than seven or eight, standing on the other side of the ditch staring at something in his garden. He was looking worried, and as Joe watched, the boy climbed over the fence and onto the rotten bridge that his uncle had made him nearly thirty years ago.

'No, no, no, you'll fall in the nettles,' he muttered. He'd meant to cut them back—meant to do all sorts of things, but between work and the baby business he'd had no time for anything.

He shot his chair back and went outside, reaching the edge of the ditch at the same time as the boy.

He wobbled and would have fallen if Joe hadn't caught him by his T-shirt and hauled him to safety off the rickety bridge.

'Are you OK?' he asked, and the boy nodded, looking worried and a bit scared.

'I didn't mean to disturb you. I was just worried about the squirrel.'

'Squirrel?'

'Yes—it's stuck in the bird feeder. I've been

watching it for ages, and it can't get out, so I was going to climb up the tree and help it.'

He shook his head. 'No. They bite. Let's have a look.'

They went round to the other side of the tree to the hugely expensive fat ball feeder that he'd restocked only that morning. Supposedly squirrel proof, only not, apparently, and most of the fat balls seemed to be inside the squirrel. It had worked its way half-out, but was stuck and struggling through a hole that seemed impossibly small.

'Hello, squirrel,' he said softly. 'You're in a bit of a mess, aren't you? It's a good job this young man spotted you. I'm Joe, by the way,' he said, turning back to the boy.

'I'm Oscar. Will you kill it?'

'No, of course not. We'll have to get it out, won't we?'

It took thick gloves, a pair of pliers and some doing, but by the time he'd unhooked the feeder, taken the lid off and dodged the teeth of the hissing, terrified squirrel, it had managed to wriggle its way free and shot off across the lawn and up the oak tree.

CAROLINE ANDERSON 239

He pulled off his gloves, turned to Oscar and gave him a high five. 'Well, done, you. I'm glad you found him. Now I'd better get you home to your mother.'

'She's at work,' he said glumly. 'She works from home, but sometimes she has to go to the office but that's OK, I can look after myself. I've got a key and she's not out for long.'

'Shouldn't you be at school?'

He shook his head. 'No. It's a training day for the teachers.'

He nodded. His aunt had worked part time, too, but he'd gone with her to her surgery and played in the waiting room under the eye of the reception staff when he'd been young. Not everyone had that opportunity. 'Have you got any brothers or sisters?'

'No. Just me.'

And he was lonely, just as Joe had been lonely. He'd spent hours alone in the playground across the ditch, idly kicking a ball around or pretending to be an explorer, and he could see that loneliness in Oscar's eyes. At least he knew his donor children all had siblings. That was one of the fears he'd nurtured needlessly all these years. Except his little daughter, safe inside Iona for now, but what would become of her? Would she go to Isla, or would Iona bring her up as an only child?

His heart squeezed, and he looked down at Oscar and smiled gently.

'I tell you what, it's lunchtime. Why don't we make a sandwich and go and eat it in the play-ground? And maybe someone will come who you can play with. You can tell them all about the squirrel.'

He went back to work, but the look in Oscar's eyes stayed with him for the rest of the day. Was that what was in store for Iona's baby? To be the only child of a working mother? He couldn't stand back and let that happen, and maybe it wasn't necessary. Maybe—if he could just shelve his doubts and dare to trust himself not to let her down as he had Natalie, to love her and cher-ish her and care for her as she deserved—they could do this together?

Keep the baby, and maybe have another one further down the line?

Was that too much to hope for? Right then it

seemed like an impossible dream, such an out-side chance that even the most desperate gam-bler wouldn't bet on it.

And he didn't believe in miracles.

They wanted it.

Isla and Steve's baby was all right, the bleed had been very minor and was nothing to worry about, just a slightly low placenta, but it was fine, she should go to term, and they'd made the decision to have Iona's baby, too.

'We'll bring them up as twins,' Isla said, her voice filled with enthusiasm. 'It'll be amazing. This baby was such an outside chance, and who knows if I'll ever have another, so twins would be just perfect and we'd never have to worry about having another one or it being an only child. And neither of us wants that. Does that make sense to you? I can't imagine growing up without you there by my side every step of the way, and our babies will have that. It'll be per-fect!'

Perfect? Iona waited for the flood of relief, but it didn't come. Instead there was a wrenching feeling of loss, and she had to swallow hard.

'Are you sure? It's a lot to take on, two babies at the same time—and of course they won't really be twins, not like we were. We knew each other long before we were born, and these two won't. They won't even share a birthday, yours will be born after mine.'

Mine? Could she still say that?

'Only a little, just a few weeks, and they'll share everything. He'll soon catch up.'

He...

Her breath caught. 'It's a boy?'

'Yes—yes, we didn't want to find out, really, but they did a 4D scan, a video, and he was wiggling around and it was so clear—he's gorgeous, Iona. It's such a miracle.'

Iona shut her eyes, and a tear squeezed out and ran down her face. She swiped it away. 'It is. It's wonderful. I'm so happy for you.' Another tear, another wipe. 'Look, I'm at work right now. Can I call you later?'

'Yes, of course. I've sent you a picture. He's the image of Steve.'

Oh, lord. She hung up, just as her phone pinged, and she opened the picture. Isla was right. Even as tiny as he was, she could see Steve in him.

Does my baby look like Joe?

'It's not my baby,' she gritted under her breath, and then she heard Joe's voice in the corridor and walked out of the locker room.

'Can we talk?' He searched her face and she avoided his eyes.

'Here?'

She shook her head. 'No. Yours, later?'

He nodded. 'I'll call when I'm finished.'

They wanted the baby, to bring them up as twins.

He waited for the flood of relief, and it didn't come, its place taken by a hollow ache that took his breath away for a moment.

'Are you OK with that?' he asked gruffly, struggling with a lump in his throat.

She shrugged. 'I have to be. What else can I do?'

'Keep it?'

She shook her head. 'No. It would be career suicide. I don't want to be a GP, I want to work in hospital medicine and they're not compatible, not at my level. I'm years from being able to do that.'

He nodded, knowing she was right, knowing it

made sense as far as her career was concerned, and at least his fear about the baby being the only child of a working mother was put to bed, but she didn't look convinced.

'So what's wrong, then?' he asked, and she shrugged.

'They won't be twins like we were, she won't be theirs, they won't love her the same as him, they can't...'

He pulled her into his arms, cradling her against his chest. 'They'll nearly be twins, and you were twins. It's better than her being an only child. She won't be lonely.' *Like me. Like Oscar. But would she truly be loved?* 'It'll be fine, Iona,' he said firmly, as much to himself as to her, 'and the baby will be part of you, so how could they fail to love her? Of course they will.'

But not as much as he and Iona would have done. How could they? But it wasn't his business. He'd told himself that over and over again, and although he couldn't have stood by and seen her struggle alone, that wasn't going to happen now, so it was back to what he'd signed up to, giving her a baby for Isla and Steve. That job was done, and it wasn't his job to worry about how they'd cope with two tiny babies at once.

Not my baby, and definitely not our *baby.*

But then the baby kicked him and he dropped his arms and stepped away. 'Are you OK with pizza? I think it's about the only thing left in the freezer—or we could go to the pub.'

Except they hadn't been to the pub since she'd had a bump, and he didn't want to have to explain their complicated arrangement to Maureen.

'Pizza's fine,' she said, to his relief.

'Are you staying over?'

She met his eyes then, for the first time in minutes, and he could see the wariness, the doubt in them.

'Am I welcome?'

'Of course you're welcome,' he said, although it wasn't strictly true. He wasn't sure he could cope with taking her to bed and making love to her, not with three of them in the bed. And the baby was really impossible to ignore now. But he'd missed her.

Missed her company, her sassiness, her warmth. Her body, but that wasn't really his for the taking any longer. It was weeks since he'd touched her, but to touch her was to remind himself over and over of the baby whose fate had seemed so uncertain and insecure. It had been easier to ignore it, but he'd made it harder for Iona and that was wrong of him. She needed his support now more than ever, and he hadn't given it to her.

'Of course you're welcome,' he repeated, his voice softer now. 'Come here.' He held out his arms and she moved into them, resting her head on his chest with a ragged sigh.

'I thought you didn't want me anymore.'

She'd said it lightly, but he felt a stab of guilt and tightened his arms around her, dropping a kiss on her hair. 'Of course I want you. I've just been buried in work. I'm sorry. I didn't mean to neglect you.'

She straightened up and smiled at him, her hand cradling his jaw, her fingers gentle. 'Don't apologise. Just talk to me from time to time, keep me in the loop. I do understand about your work.'

Even if she didn't like it. She didn't say that, but then she didn't need to, and he realised that without the baby she wouldn't have needed to contact him and he could have lost her, driven her away. And he didn't want to lose her. Ever...

Where had that come from?

He sucked in a breath, took a step away from her and opened the freezer door.

Did he really want her? She didn't know, but then after they'd eaten they sat out on the veranda, and he put his arm around her and she rested her head on his chest as they watched the sun set in a cloudless blue sky.

Summer was coming. She only had nine weeks now until her baby was due, and she felt a shiver of dread because that would be the end for her, the last act, the last time she'd have with her baby before she gave her to Isla.

She felt a little shudder go through her, and Joe must have picked it up because he looked down at her. 'You're cold. Let's go to bed.'

It wasn't late—positively early by his standards—but she wasn't going to argue. Her feet ached, the ligaments in her pelvis were starting to soften and bed seemed like a fine idea.

Especially with Joe.

Would he make love to her?

Yes. She knew that as soon as he closed the bedroom door and reached for her, his hands gentle as he undressed her. He frowned slightly but it was touched with a smile, a sort of wonder. 'Your body's changed.'

'Well, it will have done. I'm thirty one weeks now, Joe.'

The smile went, leaving just the frown. 'So soon? Where did it go?'

She laughed at that. 'Joe, you've buried yourself alive for the last few weeks. I've hardly even seen you at work.'

'I know. I'm sorry, I didn't mean to do that, it just sort of happened.'

His hands traced her body, cupping her breasts gently, feeling the weight of them, his thumbs brushing her nipples lightly, making them peak. A tiny bead appeared at the tip of one, and his thumb brushed it away.

'Wow.'

She swallowed. 'I know. I'll have to have drugs to dry up the milk.'

'Oh, Iona.' He drew her into his arms, his hug gentle, and then he let her go, threw back the covers and walked to the door. 'Get into bed. I'll be back in a minute.'

'Where are you going?'

He hesitated, and she suddenly realised what he was doing. Taking care of the need she could see in his eyes.

'Don't,' she whispered, and patted the bed beside her. 'Don't do that. Stay. Make love to me.'

'Really?'

'Really.'

He swallowed, then closed the door again, pulled off his clothes and lay down, drawing the bedclothes over them. 'I don't want to hurt you.'

'You won't hurt me. You've never hurt me.'

She shifted closer, reaching out her hand and cradling his jaw in her palm. She could feel the muscle there working, the clenching of his jaw, and she slid her hand behind his neck and drew his face down to hers, meeting his mouth with a tender kiss. 'Touch me, Joe. I won't break, and I need you. Make love to me.'

He lay awake long after she'd fallen asleep in his arms.

He'd been gentle, taken it slowly, but even so

the passion, the need, had swamped him, culminating in a climax so intense that it had shaken him to his foundations.

Because he loved her.

He blinked away the tears that welled suddenly in his eyes. No. He couldn't love her—and he certainly couldn't tell her. Not now, now her baby was destined for another life that didn't include him.

Or could he? Was it too late to stop her giving the baby away? Could they halt the whole process and keep it? Keep her, their tiny, precious daughter?

No. Not because of Isla, but because of Iona herself. She'd been worried for the child, of course, because that was who and what she was, but she'd said so many times that there was no place for a child in her life now, and not for years. He'd said the same, meant it just as much, but now, faced with this, he knew he'd been wrong.

He wanted this, wanted Iona. Wanted the baby, more than he'd ever known he could want anything, but he couldn't have her. She wasn't his to want or need, and in just a few short weeks she'd be out of his life for ever, barring the odd photograph or Christmas card. Out of Iona's, too, and any dreams he might have cherished of them becoming a family had just gone out of the window.

I can't lose both my girls...

He felt a wave of grief so intense he almost cried out. Maybe he did, because Iona stirred beside him, shifting her body slightly so that her leg lay over his, pinning him down and cutting off any hope of slipping out of bed and escaping to the study to immerse himself in something he could cope with, something he had a hope of influencing.

And so he lay there, and he held her in his arms and tried to imprint the memory on his heart, and eventually she rolled away and he made his escape.

'Have you been here all night?'

He was sprawled on the sofa in the study, his laptop upside down on the floor where it must have landed, and he opened his eyes, blinked, and sat up, stretching stiffly.

'Yeah—maybe. I don't know, I can't remember. Where's my laptop?'

'On the floor.'

He picked it up, swore softly and opened it, then sighed and closed it again.

'It looks all right. It's solid state, so dropping it shouldn't have messed it up.' He scrubbed a hand through his hair and looked at his wrist.

'It's six o'clock. I thought I should wake you. I'm going to go home and get ready for work and you probably need to do the same.' She hesitated, then said, 'Will I see you later?'

His eyes met hers, and she could see a whole world of conflicting emotions in them.

'Don't worry. Just let me know.'

'No. Come. Stay. I'll do a food order.'

She smiled. 'Well, that might be an idea if we aren't going to starve to death. I've left you the last two bits of bread so you can have breakfast.'

She walked over to him and he stood up, put his arms round her and hugged her gently.

'Thanks,' he mumbled through her hair. 'I'm sorry you felt abandoned. I should have realised. I won't let it happen again.'

'Don't be silly. I'm fine. I'll see you later.' She eased away from him, pressed a kiss to his stubbled cheek and left him to it, wishing she could believe that guilty promise.

She found out she could believe it, and although he was still ridiculously busy, he made time for her whenever he could. They got into a pattern, then, of getting together when their shifts aligned, and the weeks ticked slowly by.

She was getting more awkward, finding work more tiring, but the closer she got to her due date, the less she wanted to stop because then she'd have nothing to do but think about what was to come.

And she didn't want to think about it. Didn't want to think about the time when the baby was gone and she couldn't play happy families with Joe any longer. Couldn't pretend to herself that she was going to bring her baby home to him, to the little room beside his bedroom that would make a perfect nursery.

Couldn't pretend that she'd sit on the veranda rocking the baby to sleep in her pram, or take her for walks along the country lanes, or take her to the playground to explore the sand in the sandpit or crawl over the grass in the garden and discover the smell and the taste and the feel of it beneath her chubby fingers.

That was for Isla to do, Isla and Steve and their little miracle baby.

And she—she had her career to focus on, her future to plan, her life to map out. A life without Joe, without the baby. She could hardly bring herself to think about it, but she didn't have to now.

Not yet. For now she had them both, and she was going to cherish every moment of it.

And then, when she was thirty nine weeks pregnant, everything changed.

CHAPTER TEN

HE'D MISSED A call from Iona, but she'd left a voicemail.

'I've had a show. Call me when you get this.'

He felt his heart kick into overdrive and rang her instantly.

'Where are you?'

'At work, so I can't talk for long. I'm fine, it wasn't much, but I think I'm getting close. I've called Isla and Steve and warned them. They're coming down. I thought they could stay at my flat and I could stay with you. Is that OK? Just until—you know.'

He did know. He knew only too well, and it was all he'd been able to think about for weeks, but at least he'd got the last course out of the way, and he'd sat the final exam a week ago. Anything else could wait because there was no way he could abandon her now.

'Yes, of course it's OK,' he said, although his

head was screaming *No!* at the top of its voice, but that was just self-preservation and he ignored it. 'Do you think you should go home now?'

'No, I haven't even had a twinge yet. It could be days. I've told James I'll be on mat leave from the end of today, so I'll finish my shift and go and sort the flat. They won't be down here till this evening, Steve's got a meeting with a client at three and then they'll set off.'

He swallowed. 'OK. Well, ring me if anything changes. I'll be home by six.'

'Are you sure? That's early for you.'

'Yes, I'm sure.' He'd make damn sure, because this wasn't something that could wait. When Iona went into labour, she would have Isla with her and maybe Steve, but not now, while she was waiting. Not yet.

For now, she'd only have him, and he'd have her. What happened after that only time would tell, but he was going to be here for her now if it was the last thing he did.

He went and found his consultant and told him he needed a week off, starting now.

'Now?'

'Yes—well, from six this evening. I'm sorry,

I know it's difficult, but—there's something I have to do. Something personal. And it won't happen again.'

His boss searched his eyes, then nodded as if he'd found what he was looking for. 'OK. Well, if you must.'

'I must.'

'Fine. Keep in touch.'

'Of course.'

She wasn't sure how she got through the rest of the day, but when she went off at the end of her shift, it felt surreal.

How could she go off on maternity leave when she wasn't going to be a mother? There should be another word…

Isla and Steve arrived at six thirty, and she let them in, hugged them and gave them keys. 'Libby's away on holiday at the moment so you'll have the place to yourselves and you can come and go whenever you like. There's unrestricted parking on the street, and if you can't find anything, just ring me and I can probably tell you where you might find it. And there's milk and butter in the fridge, and some bread on the side there, and various other bits and pieces. Just help yourselves.'

She hugged them again, kissed Isla goodbye and walked carefully down the stairs. Steve carried her bag down and put it in the car, and hugged her again.

'We're so excited,' he said. 'Our first baby. We can't believe it's actually happening.'

'No, nor can I,' she murmured, dredged up a smile, got awkwardly behind the wheel and drove away before she did something stupid like cry.

Joe was home when she arrived, and she walked through the door and straight into his arms.

'Are you OK?'

She nodded, even though she wasn't. 'Mmm. They're here, in my flat. I've told them to ring if they need me for anything.'

'Where's your bag?'

'In the car.'

'I'll get it. Go and sit down and put your feet up. You look done in.'

Did she? She didn't feel it—didn't feel much of anything, except edgy. But she did as he said, kicking off her shoes and settling down in the corner of the sofa with her feet up. The baby wriggled, settling herself into a better position, and she stroked her lovingly, feeling the curve of the baby's spine, the little bump of her bottom, the jut of her heel.

'It's OK, baby,' she murmured. 'You stay there, you hear me? There's no hurry. You take as long as you like.'

'Cup of tea?'

She looked up and saw Joe standing in the doorway, watching her with a strange expression on his face. And for the first time in ages she couldn't read his eyes.

'That would be lovely. Decaf, please.'

He rolled his eyes and walked into the kitchen. She could see him through the double doors, pottering quietly. Emptying the dishwasher, finding mugs, putting shopping away. He must have done an internet order, she realised, or a lightning trolley-dash.

'I ordered some food, things with longish dates so we don't have to worry about shopping,' he said, coming in with the tea and settling down at the other end of the sofa. 'How are you feeling? Any change?'

She shook her head. 'No, not really. I don't feel any different. I hope it's not a false alarm and Isla and Steve aren't hanging around indefinitely.' Which was a lie, because the longer it was, the longer the baby would be with her, the longer she could pretend...

He picked up his tea and rested his other hand over her feet, stroking them absently. 'How's Isla?'

'Oh, OK, I think. She looks a bit thin. I think pregnancy's been tough on her. She hasn't felt great. It makes me realise I've come off lightly.' Except of course at the end of it Isla would have two babies, and she'd have none...

He was watching her thoughtfully, as if he could see straight through her, and she turned her attention to the tea. 'So what's for supper?' she asked, changing the subject.

'Whatever you fancy. I got a fish pie and some sugar snap peas, or you could have pea and ham risotto, or—'

'Fish pie sounds nice. Does it need long in the oven?'

He shook his head and got to his feet. 'I'll put it in now. I might as well feed you up while you're not in active labour.'

That again. She felt the baby kick and her hand went instinctively to the bump, soothing her with gentle strokes.

Joe turned on the oven, took the fish pie back out of the fridge and glanced at Iona through the glass doors. She was stroking the baby, and her expression twisted something deep inside him. He'd seen it before, on the faces of women stoically tending their loved ones when all hope was gone. Grief—carefully masked, hidden from everyone except those who knew, every caress a tender farewell.

He rested his hands on the edge of the worktop, dropped his head forward and took several long, slow deep breaths.

He was dreading this. Dreading the moment when she'd tell him that she was in labour, dreading the moment of birth—dreading the moment their child ceased to be theirs, and became someone else's daughter.

Breathe...

* * *

He sent her to bed early before it was even dark, and she had a shower and washed and dried her hair, just in case. He followed her up shortly afterwards, and as he got into bed she turned to face him and snuggled up close, resting her top leg over his to ease the ache in her pelvis, her head on his chest, his heart beating steadily under her ear.

'You OK?' he asked, his voice a rumble in his chest.

'Mmm. Just—you know.'

Maybe he did, because his grip tightened and he held her closer. 'Oh, sweetheart. Are you going to be OK?'

She shrugged helplessly. 'I don't know. I don't know how I'll feel when I—you know. Hand her over...'

Her voice cracked and she sucked in a breath, and his lips touched her forehead. 'I'll be there for you. You know that.'

'I do. Thank you. I just wish...'

'Wish?'

'That I'd met you before.'

'Before—?'

'Before Natalie. Before Dan, when we were both bright and shiny and fresh out of the box instead of—I don't know. Tarnished.'

'Tarnished. That's a good word for it.' He let out a long, slow breath, his chest sinking beneath her ear. 'Do you think—?'

'What?'

'No, it's just a crazy dream. Only—when we first found out they were having a baby, I thought maybe we—well, whatever, they're having her so it doesn't matter anymore.'

His voice seemed to break a little on that last word, and she tilted her head and studied his face in the dim light filtering through the blind. His jaw was clenched, his eyes open and staring fixedly at the ceiling, and the light caught a tiny trickle running from the outer corner of his eye.

'Oh, Joe. Do you think we could have made it work? You, me, our baby? Or would I just have held you back?'

'You wouldn't have held me back. Never think that. You've been amazing, this whole hellish year, but I've got there, I've done everything I needed to do, and now I just have to wait—so, no, you wouldn't have held me back. You haven't. And—I don't know, maybe it's still just a crazy dream, but perhaps, when this is all over and we're in a better place, maybe we can give ourselves a chance.'

Could they? Was there really a chance for them when this was done, when their little girl had been handed over and they'd got over the wrenching loss she knew they'd feel—would there be a chance for them?

She squeezed her eyes tight shut. Oh, she hoped so. But in the meantime he was here with her, and so was their baby, and she needed rest. She was exhausted, and the next few days and weeks would be an emotional rollercoaster.

'Go to sleep, my love,' he murmured, as if he'd read her mind.

His hand stroked her back slowly, rhythmically, soothing away her tangled feelings, and feeling safe, cocooned from reality, she drifted off to sleep.

Her phone woke them a few hours later, and he reached over her and picked it up.

'It's Steve,' he said, handing it to her, and her heart started to pound.

'Hi, Steve, what's up?'

'Isla's waters have broken and she's having really strong contractions, so I've called an ambulance,' he said, his voice shaking. 'Can you come to the hospital? I wouldn't ask but we don't know anyone there and it's too soon and—'

'Steve, it's fine, I'm on my way. I'll meet you there. Call me when you arrive and give her my love. It'll be OK.'

She pressed the phone to her chest and turned to Joe, but he was out of bed, getting dressed.

'Did you hear that?'

He nodded. 'Get dressed, I'm coming with you.'

'Are you sure? What about work tomorrow—today, whatever it is?'

'I'm not working the weekend anyway, and I've taken a week off so I could be there for you, and I will, no matter what happens. Come on. It's OK. She'll be all right.'

'You can't know that,' she said, struggling into her underwear. 'What if—?'

'Don't do the what-ifs, Iona. Just deal with it as it comes, hour by hour, day by day.'

She pulled her dress over her head and searched his eyes. 'Is that what you're doing?'

He looked away. 'Yes. I've been doing it for weeks—months. How do you think I got through all the revision and courses?'

He was talking about work. Or was he...?

She found her shoes, wriggled her feet into them and stood up, grabbing her phone off the bed.

'OK, let's go.'

Isla's baby was born half an hour after they arrived at the hospital, weighing a mere three and a half pounds, and he was taken immediately to NICU.

'Go with him,' Isla begged, so Steve went, and Joe went with him, leaving Iona with Isla.

'You'll have to wait until the paediatrician's assessed him,' they were told, so Joe told Steve to go back to Isla.

'I'll call you the minute you can go in,' he promised, and as soon as Steve was gone, he buzzed and they let him in. No point in not pulling rank. He'd see what he could find out...

* * *

'How is he?'

'OK.' He sat down beside her, and he looked drained.

'What's wrong? Is there something wrong?'

'No. Not now, but he needed two umbilical lines.'

'And?'

'And the consultant was busy with another baby, the IR was tied up as well and the registrar was struggling and about to put in two peripheral lines instead.'

'So you did it?'

He nodded. 'Well, I have just done a refresher course on venous and arterial access in neonates, and it was only building on what I already know and do all the time, but I was feeling the stress by the end of it. They couldn't measure his blood gases without it, though, or get any drugs into him, so it was pretty critical, but it's so delicate, the tissues are really fragile and he seems so tiny. Still, it was working, so hopefully he'll be all right now. How's Isla?'

'In bits. She hardly had time to hold him before he was whisked away. I don't think she's stopped crying.' She closed her eyes and rested her head against him. 'Is he going to be all right?'

'I hope so. He's small, but he's holding his own at the moment and breathing by himself so it's looking hopeful. And thirty two weeks isn't that young, not in the great scheme of things. How are you?'

His voice was soft, his arm around her shoulders, and she wanted to lean into him and cry, but she didn't. She straightened up and met his eyes. 'I'm shattered. I really need to go back to bed, but I don't like to leave them.'

'They're in good hands, and we won't be far away,' he pointed out, and she nodded.

'Yes, you're right.' She rubbed her arms with her hands, not because she was cold but just—

'Hey, come on. Let's get you back to bed. You can call them from the car. The staff will look after them, they're used to this. You need to rest.'

Over the next forty eight hours baby William made slow but steady progress, with Isla and Steve spending all day with him, taking it in turns to sleep.

Iona visited them again on Monday morning,

but they were so focused, so preoccupied by their tiny, frail son that they barely noticed she was there. It was as if they'd forgotten why they were there in the first place, and Isla's fears about her own baby being second best were starting to overwhelm her.

But what could she do? They'd been so adamant about having both, bringing them up as twins. She couldn't turn round to them now, just because things hadn't gone according to plan, and tell them they couldn't have their baby.

Although if Joe had shown the slightest sign of wanting to keep her, had said or done anything to indicate he had any feelings for her, then she might have voiced her fears. But he hadn't, almost the opposite—apart from that one occasion, when he'd felt the baby move for the first time and had scooted down the bed and kissed her bump and murmured, 'Hello, you,' his voice so full of tenderness and wonder. And the night Isla had gone into labour, when he'd held her and wondered if they could have made a go of it, or if they might have a chance together later on, when they were in a better place.

That didn't mean he was ready to sign up for

parenthood now, though, and without his support she wouldn't be able to keep her baby. What kind of a life would that be for either of them? And if Isla and Steve had her, she'd still be able to see her, to love her, to shower her with gifts and cuddles and kisses, but she'd have two loving, supportive parents instead of one stressed mother who was trying to juggle her work and childcare commitments against ridiculous odds.

That surely was the better option—at least for the baby?

She rubbed her bump, hoping she would stay tucked up there inside her for a little while longer, just until William was out of the woods and his parents had the time and the emotion to cope with the arrival of another baby. And maybe by then, she'd be ready to do what she knew in her heart she had to do...

Her agonising wait wasn't lost on Joe. She looked strained and exhausted, so strung out by the knowledge of what was to come that he was worried about her. And he knew what she was feeling. It was in her eyes, in her body language—and in his heart, slowly shredding it to pieces.

Please let the baby stay there a bit longer, just until William's stronger and they can do this. Please don't make it harder than it already is.

But whoever was in charge obviously wasn't listening, because she went into labour that night.

He drove her to the hospital at three on Tuesday morning, when her contractions were coming every three minutes and getting so strong she could hardly breathe through them.

'I can't do this,' she said when he'd parked the car, and he took her hand and squeezed it gently.

'Yes, you can. You've come this far, you can make it.'

She shook her head. 'I can't, Joe. I'm not brave enough. Everyone tells me I'm brave, but I'm not brave, not at all.'

'Of course you are,' he murmured, his voice full of a conviction she didn't feel. 'You're doing something most women would find impossible, and through it all you've been strong. If that isn't courage, I don't know what is.'

She didn't know, either, but it wasn't courage. She felt trapped, trapped into a situation they'd never foreseen, trapped into giving away a daughter she already loved more than anything in the world when it didn't seem necessary any more. At least not for Isla and Steve, and maybe not for her. Would being a GP be worse than giving away her child? No, of course it wouldn't, but how could she tell them she'd changed her mind?

And it wouldn't be fair on Joe, who she knew would feel obliged to support her even though she'd never ever ask him to.

Another contraction gripped her body, bringing the moment of truth closer, and she bit her lips and tried to breathe through it.

'OK?'

'No. I'm not OK, and I don't feel strong now, not at all. I feel scared.' Not of the physical pain. That paled into insignificance compared to what was coming.

'Oh, Iona.' He held her silently in his arms, not even trying to comfort her, because he must realise that nothing he could say could change any of what was coming, and she knew he was feeling it, too. Poor Joe. It was never meant to be like this…

She had another contraction, stronger than the others, and when it passed he got out of the car, went round and opened her door. 'Come on, we need to get you inside,' he said gently, but when they got up to Maternity they were told Isla was sleeping in the parents' room off the ward, and Steve had just gone home to Iona's flat to catch a couple of hours, so they were alone.

And she couldn't do this alone.

'Stay with me?' she asked, and he hesitated because that had never been the plan and she'd given him no warning, no time to shore up his defences.

Not that it would have worked. And she was trying so hard not to beg, but he searched her eyes and she was sure he could see it, the fear, the desperation. Not of the labour, but of that moment afterwards when she gave away the most precious thing in the world…

She saw the moment he caved, saw the moment the shutters came down in his eyes, and she almost wished she hadn't asked him.

'Of course I will,' he said, burying his feelings and hoping he could do this, could stay with her and support her while she gave birth to the child they couldn't keep.

This is wrong! his heart was screaming, but he stayed by her side, held her, rocked her, talked to her in between contractions, trying to reassure her and support her in doing what she'd set out to do, to help to make it easier for her. So he parroted all the old mantras he'd been drumming into himself for weeks.

Lies, all of it.

It'll be all right. They'll love her, of course they will. You'll be fine. She'll be fine. I'm here, I'm not going anywhere.

That last bit was the only one that was true, the only promise he could guarantee.

And then at last their daughter was born, tiny and perfect, and he stepped back away from the bed, the heart-stopping sound as she gave her first cry tearing him apart, and he knew that promise, too, had been a lie. He wouldn't be there. He couldn't. Not for her, or for the baby. Not when she gave their perfect, beautiful little daughter away.

It was Liv, the midwife who'd been so supportive, so understanding, who picked her up, Liv who laid her on Iona's chest, Liv who smiled and patted the baby dry with a warm towel.

He couldn't take his eyes off her, off the shock of dark hair, the tiny fingers, the skinny little legs, but he couldn't watch, either, and he took another step back and hit the wall.

He sucked in a breath. How could it hurt so much?

'I'll get Isla,' he said, his voice strangled, but Iona reached out her hand.

'No! Not yet, please. Stay with me. Liv can get her later, Joe. Stay with me now, please? Just for a little longer...'

So he stayed, against his better judgement, while Liv did her job quietly and unobtrusively, and he watched as Iona held her baby and stroked her tenderly, every touch, every stroke cutting him to the quick. What was it doing to her, this brave, beautiful woman who could sacrifice herself like this?

Then finally everything was done, and Liv turned to them, her face full of compassion.

'Do you want me to fetch them yet, or would you like some time alone together?'

'Please,' he said, because he wasn't ready. He'd never be ready. But Iona shook her head.

'Get them, please. We have to do this, and the longer we wait, the harder it'll be.'

The door closed softly behind Liv, and Iona looked up at him, her eyes welling with tears.

'Stay with me, Joe? Help me do this? I can't do it on my own—'

She was crying now, tears streaming down her cheeks, and he had to blink really hard to focus.

'I can't,' he said, every word feeling as if it was wrenched from him. 'I can't watch you give our daughter away, Iona, I just can't. I know you have to, I know you've promised and you'll never break that promise, no matter how much it hurts you, but I'm not as brave as you. Don't make me part of it, please.'

He couldn't see now, his tears welling too fast, but then he blinked, his head bent, and the baby's eyes were fixed on him. Her little arm moved, lifting up—reaching out to him?—and the last piece of his heart cracked and fell in two.

'Oh, baby...' He held out his hand to her, and her tiny fingers curled around his fingertip, her grip strong and fierce. So like her mother. So brave, so strong. Blinded by tears, and carefully, so as not to hurt her, he unfurled those tiny fingers one by one and pulled his hand away.

It was breaking his heart.

She could see it in every line of his body, every word he spoke, the pain in his eyes so raw it was flaying her alive, and she caught his hand, gripping it tightly.

'Oh, Joe. I'm so, so sorry. I never meant this to hurt you. It was supposed to be simple, but it isn't, is it? None of it. I've got no choice, but I can't do this to you, too, so of course you can go, my love. Just promise me one thing. Come back to me, when I've done it?' she begged, her voice cracking as she gave up the fight to hide her feelings. 'It's going to kill me to give her away, and I can't lose you, too. Don't do that to me.'

He lifted her hand to his lips, clinging to it like a lifeline.

'I won't leave you,' he promised, his voice as unsteady as hers. 'I can't, I love you far too much and I never expected to feel like that. If I'd only done what I was meant to do that night, if I hadn't made love to you, then maybe this wouldn't have happened, maybe I wouldn't have let myself fall in love with you and pretend that it was all going to be all right, because it isn't...'

His voice cracked, and he ground to a halt, squeezing his eyes shut to stop the tears from falling, but they were falling anyway and she watched them and realised everything he'd said was true. He wasn't lying, he wasn't saying what he thought she'd want to hear to make it possible for her to keep their baby.

He was telling her the raw, unvarnished truth, and it was killing him.

'Why didn't you tell me?' Iona asked, her heart breaking for him. 'I've loved you for so long now. Why didn't you tell me that you love me?'

'Because I didn't know! I didn't dare to let myself think about it, but now I have it's so blindingly obvious, and I know it doesn't change anything, because I know you won't break your promise to Isla. And they'll be great parents, I know that, and I know she'll be happy, and I know she'll be loved, and we can still see her, maybe later when it's stopped hurting quite so much. And maybe then, when we're both ready, when you've finished your training and I've got my consultancy and the pain isn't so raw still, maybe we can do this again—start our own family. Have another baby, just for us.

'And I won't go now. I can't. I'll stay with you, and I'll watch while the thing I want most in the world is taken away from us, because I can't let you do that alone, and especially not when they don't even need her. It just seems so wrong...'

He ground to a halt and heard a faint sound behind him, a quiet sob. A hand touched his shoulder and he turned his head, to find Isla and Steve standing behind him, arms round each other, their faces drenched with tears.

'It is wrong,' Isla said brokenly, stumbling to Iona's side and taking her hand, gripping it with both of hers. 'Of course it's wrong, and we wouldn't *dream* of taking her from you now, not now we know how you feel. We didn't know you were in love, we thought you were just friends, and if we'd had the slightest clue that you wanted her so much, we'd never have said we'd still take her, even without me being pregnant. How could we hurt you like that?

'When we talked about it first we had no idea what it meant to love a child, and then when we found out I was pregnant, how could we tell you we didn't want your baby when you done all this just for us? But now—now we've had William, just the thought of losing him, of giving him away—it would break our hearts, Iona, just like it's breaking yours. We couldn't do that to you. To either of you.'

'But—I thought you wanted twins?' Iona said, but Joe could see the hope dawning in her face, the love for her baby shining in her eyes, and he pressed his hand over his mouth, holding down the emotion that was threatening to swamp him, not daring to believe that it might all come right.

Isla shook her head. 'No. It was the only solution we could think of, and we would have done it willingly. That's why we're here. We were coming to tell you we'd take her if that was what you really wanted, but it's so obvious you both love her, and she belongs with you—

with both of you, and that's where she should be, with her own mother and father, and I can't think of any two people who deserve it more than you. So keep her, and love her, and I know you'll be happy.'

She kissed Iona, touched the baby with a loving hand and then left in Steve's arms, and Joe gave up the fight against his tears, gathered Iona and the baby up against his heart and wept.

Be happy?

Iona, sitting outside on the veranda while Joe fiddled in the kitchen, didn't know when she'd ever been this happy. And she'd never, ever seen Joe smile the way he was today.

It might have been because he'd had a phone call from his clinical lead offering him the consultancy, but she didn't think so. Or, at least, not just because of that.

He brought out a cake—her mother's apple cake recipe, which he'd stolen—and put it and a pot of tea safely out of the way on the table.

'She's got your eyes,' she told him, and he smiled and sat down beside her, looking down at his daughter with so much love it made her heart squeeze.

'Yes, I noticed. It's like looking in a mirror, only rather prettier.'

'Well, that's not hard,' she teased, and he gave a quiet chuckle and hugged her to his side. Then he gave her a thoughtful look and shifted so he could see her better.

'I want to ask you something, but I'm only going to ask it if you'll say yes,' he said.

'Will I regret it?'

He smiled a little sadly. 'I hope not.' And then before she realised what he was doing, he was kneeling in front of her, holding her hand in his and staring intently into her eyes.

She stared back, searching them and seeing everything she'd ever dreamed of, and she felt the smile start deep inside her and spread until she was smiling everywhere.

'Yes,' she said, before he could open his mouth.

'Yes, what?'

'Yes, I'll marry you,' she said softly. 'Will you marry me? Will you love, honour, and cherish me, and keep yourself only for me, as long as we both live?'

'Yes,' he said, his voice gruff and uneven. 'Oh, Iona—yes, I will. Now and for ever. I love you so much—'

'I love you, too,' she murmured gently, her hand reaching up and caressing his rugged cheek as he wrapped her and the baby carefully in his arms. 'I never thought I'd feel like this again. Well, no, not again, perhaps, because I've never felt like this before. It's as if suddenly everything that was wrong in my life has just shifted a bit and fallen into place, and it's all down to her— that tiny little girl, and my silly idea that babies should be conceived in love.'

He smiled and let go, sitting back down beside her again. 'I don't think it was a silly idea at all, and without it this might never have happened. And it was certainly true in her case because I fell in love with you that night,' he said softly, staring down at the baby in her arms. He reached over and lifted her carefully into his arms, his face filled with wonder. 'And look at her. Our baby. I can't believe she's here with us. I never dreamed—no, that's not true. I used to dream sometimes that we could keep her, try and convince myself we could find a way, and all the time I knew it was hopeless, but it wasn't.'

His finger traced her cheek, the line of her tiny little nose, the rosebud lips with such tenderness she felt her eyes filling just to see it.

'She's ours, Iona. She's our own little miracle, and we owe her everything, and when she's old enough, maybe we can tell her the story of how we fell in love.'

'Maybe not all of it,' she said with a smile, and he chuckled softly.

'No. Maybe not quite all…'

* * * * *

LET'S TALK

Romance

For exclusive extracts, competitions
and special offers, find us online:

f facebook.com/millsandboon

◎ @millsandboonuk

🐦 @millsandboon

Or get in touch on 0844 844 1351*

For all the latest titles coming soon,
visit millsandboon.co.uk/nextmonth

Want even more
ROMANCE?

Join our bookclub today!